Quest Chasers
THE SCREAMING
MUMMY

Grace and Thomas Lockhaven

Edited by David Aretha

TWISTED KEY
p u b l i s h i n g

2017

First Printing: 2017

ISBN 978-1-947744-02-8

Twisted Key Publishing, LLC
www.twistedkeypublishing.com

Ordering Information:
Special discounts are available on quantity purchases by corporations, associations, educators, and others. For details, contact the publisher at the above listed address.

U.S. trade bookstores and wholesalers: Please contact Twisted Key Publishing, LLC by email twistedkeypublishing@gmail.com.

"To my mom and dad. I cannot thank you enough for your constant encouragement and love. From the child with the overactive imagination and insatiable questioning mind, I thank you both with all of my heart for believing in me."

Thomas Lockhaven

To my best friend and confidant Gemma, without you my world would be flat like a pancake...without the syrup.

Grace Lockhaven

Contents

Acknowledgements

We would like to thank David Aretha, our editor, for his patience and excellent guidance. His guidance was invaluable.

Special thanks to Jelev for his artistic imagination.

Grace and Thomas Lockhaven

1

An Uninvited Guest

Tommy jolted upright in his bed. There it was again—he heard the floor creak. Someone was there. "Mom? Dad? Is that you?"

He listened intently. Nothing...

Tommy's eyes widened. *Did a shadow just pass under the door?*

He could feel the fear—like ice water—filling his veins. His breath came in shallow gasps. He watched in horror as his doorknob began to turn slowly.

"D-d-d-ad?" Tommy urgently half-whispered, half-shouted.

He rolled off his bed onto the floor. He looked around his room. There was no place to hide. He looked at his second-floor window. It was a long drop, but it was the only way out. Tommy threw open the window and kicked out the screen. It fell to the ground with a metallic clang.

A white hand appeared along the edge of his door as it opened, and a skeletal white face with dead black eyes stared back at him. An evil smile stretched across the face of the intruder. Tommy tried to scream but his words got stuck in his throat. His hands clutched the sides of his face as a sinister voice filled his head.

"I told you I would come for you, Tommy. You've seen too much."

Tommy ripped his lamp off the bedside table and hurled it at the intruder. It slammed into his face, the lightbulb shattering into slivers of glass.

As Tommy stepped backward, he could feel the rush of cold air against his neck. The creature rushed toward his prey, his skeletal hands outstretched. Tommy clambered backwards through the window, his fingertips frantically searching for the metal frame. Simultaneously he looked down for a safe place to drop some twenty feet below.

This is going to hurt, Tommy thought, but just as he began his freefall, his right arm jerked painfully upward. He cried out; it felt like his arm was being pulled out of the socket. The creature's icy-cold grip encircled his wrist—his long black nails tore into his flesh. Tommy ripped and pulled, trying to free his wrist from the creature's grasp. "Let go of me!" he screamed through gritted teeth.

Tommy dangled in the air, kicking his feet and screaming. The grip on his forearm tightened, and he felt a bone in his wrist beginning to give way. Tears of pain poured out of his eyes. The creature leaned forward, his mouth against Tommy's cheek. Tommy could feel the hot breath on his skin as the intruder whispered...

"You're not going anywhere, Tommy."

Tommy struggled, kicking hard, driving his heels forcefully against the house. Snow and ice rained down on him from the roof, and then he saw it. Glistening in the moonlight, to his left, a long icicle hung from the gutter that ran down the side of his house. Tommy kicked out with all of his might and, while swinging his body to the left, reached out and ripped the icicle off the gutter.

"Enough!" said the creature.

As Tommy kicked and struggled like an insect caught in a spider's web, he felt himself being pulled back into his room.

Suddenly, the neighbor's porchlight flashed on. The creature turned his head, and in that split-second, Tommy thrust the icicle into his captor's forearm. As if in slow motion, Tommy saw the tattered arm of his shirt clutched in the creature's hand, noticed the surprised look in the creature's eyes—and then Tommy was falling through space, arms and legs flailing as he crashed into the holly bush below.

Pain filled Tommy's body as it seemed like a hundred tiny little knives pierced and lacerated his skin. He rolled onto the ground and began screaming, "Mom! Dad!" Puffs of smoke accented every word.

Tommy pulled himself to his feet. His parents' bedroom light was on, and from outside he could hear the pounding of running feet inside the house. The front door flung open just as Tommy began racing up the front porch steps.

"Dad!" screamed Tommy.

"Tommy, what are you...?" Mr. Prescott's eyes grew wide as he saw the scrapes and cuts covering Tommy's face. His son's mouth was moving but nothing was coming out.

"Tommy, what's going on?" he said as a wave of confusion and concern filled his face. He pulled Tommy into the doorway. His mother grabbed him. "Tommy, what happened?" she exclaimed, her eyes wide with fear. "Are you OK?"

"Dad," Tommy managed. "There's a man...there's a man in my room! I jumped out the window to escape!"

"Ellie, call the police!" Tommy's dad said urgently.

Dad quickly spun around, threw open the closet door, and pulled out a baseball bat.

"Dad, he's huge! Dad, please, just wait for the police! Please, Dad, he might have a gun," Tommy begged. He knew his dad wasn't one to back down easily, and the man in his room possessed a strength that wasn't from this world.

Tommy's dad hesitated for a moment, his jaw clenched firmly. "OK," he nodded, and then rushed everyone outside onto the front lawn.

Several neighbors appeared, dressed hurriedly in pajamas and winter coats. They stood on their porches, their faces filled with curiosity and worry.

"Joe," Mr. Norris, their next-door neighbor, called out as he stepped onto his porch still pulling on his winter coat, "is everything OK?"

"There's an intruder in our house!" shouted Mr. Prescott. Within seconds, all of the neighbors disappeared behind closed doors, their faces cautiously peeking out their windows. Mr. Norris frantically motioned Tommy's family over.

"Inside, inside," said Mr. Norris, holding open the door and motioning them into his house. "Have you called the police?" he asked urgently.

"Yes," said Tommy's mom as they rushed into the safety of his house. "They'll be here any minute."

Mr. Norris ushered the three into the living room, where they could watch their house safely. Shivers raced through Tommy's body. He wasn't sure if it was from the cold or adrenaline.

Tommy withdrew inside his mind. Scattered pieces of conversation danced just on the edge of his consciousness.

Suddenly a terrifying thought hit him. "Eevie," he whispered aloud.

"Mom," he said abruptly, "I need your phone!"

Tommy grabbed the phone. His hands trembled as he punched in Eevie's number. Each ring felt like an eternity.

Tommy walked out of the room and into the hallway by the front door.

Come on, Eevie, answer! Tommy pleaded.

"Hello?" whispered a sleepy, confused voice. "Wha—"

"Eevie, listen." Tommy began to shake uncontrollably. "The ranger, he was in my room. He tried to kill me!"

"Tommy, where are you? Are you OK?" Eevie's panicked voice practically climbed through the airways and shook him by the shoulders.

"I'm safe. I'm with my parents. We're at Mr. Norris's house. Listen! Make sure that your house is locked up! Make sure every window and door is locked. If he found me, he's gonna be able to find you! …Just tell your parents that someone broke into my house! I don't have my phone, so if you need me, call my mom's phone."

Blue lights strobed and spotlights began shining on Tommy's house. The police had arrived.

"Eevie…," Tommy whispered. "He's coming for us!"

Eevie's words caught in her throat. Her heart pounded against her sternum. "I know," she exhaled. "Be careful."

"You too, Eevie. I gotta go—the police are here."

Eevie jumped out of bed and turned on all the lights. Her eyes moved toward her window, half expecting to see the ranger's black eyes staring back at her. A powerful, numbing rush of fear flooded her body. "Here we go again," she whispered aloud to herself.

Just a few months earlier, Eevie and Tommy had met the ranger at Black Hallow Park. Dozens of children had vanished over the past century, and a classmate named Drew Morris had nearly been killed by what he described as a very angry, demon-possessed tree.

Hoping to solve the mystery of the disgruntled tree, they found themselves ripped from this world and cast into a deadly cavern filled with savage traps and challenges that were meant to kill them. They survived, and now their favorite evil ranger had been sent to accelerate their demise.

2

DO I HAVE RABIES?

Over the next several hours, the police searched the house and questioned Tommy. He drew in a sharp breath when he saw his ragged shirt sleeve laying on top of his pillow.

Tommy explained how he had thrown open the window and crawled out, and the intruder had grabbed his arm just as he had let go. The forensic team took pictures of his arm where the nails of the intruder had dug into his flesh. A row of angry, purple welts dotted his wrist.

A heavyset policeman with a shock of black hair and bright red cheeks pointed at Tommy's arm. "Are those from his fingernails?" he asked in disbelief. He gently turned Tommy's arm over for a better view. "Make sure you are up-to-date on your tetanus shots." Tommy nodded and then looked down at his battered arm. *Tetanus...more like rabies.*

Tommy's father stood silently, his mouth drawn tight as he listened to the description of what had happened. A forensic investigator dressed in a white protective jumpsuit and blue latex gloves was on his knees, taking pictures of black splotches that went from the window-sill onto Tommy's floor.

"Did the intruder have some kind of liquid?" asked the investigator as he looked up at Tommy.

"No, sir. I stabbed him in the arm with an icicle. It...it must be his blood."

Out of the corner of his eye, Tommy noticed his father's knees buckle and his face go pale. His father knew something!

Tommy turned his head back to the investigator, who said, "I don't think it's his blood. It seems to be some type of acid, you see?" He pointed to the floor. "It's begun to eat into the wood."

"I didn't see anything, sir. I stabbed him with the icicle and he screamed and let me go. I never saw anything else in his hands."

The investigator pulled out a device with a razor attached to it and scraped the black, hardened liquid into a sample bag.

He stood and looked at Tommy, giving him a *don't worry* look. "We'll send this to the lab. They'll be able to tell us what it is."

The lead officer turned toward Tommy's dad. "Your son was extremely brave and lucky, Mr. Prescott. We'll leave a cruiser here tonight to watch over things, and we'll make sure we add some additional patrols over the next week until we catch this guy. If any of you hear or see *anything* suspicious, call us right away."

"Thank you," said Tommy. His own voice sounded so strange, so disconnected.

Mr. Prescott's mind seemed to be somewhere else as well—somewhere far, far away.

3

Eevie Makes a Wand-erful

Discovery

It was Friday night...well, Saturday morning. Eevie sat at her desk, unable to sleep. Every time her eyes closed, she immediately began to see the ranger's face, his eyes completely black, filled with evil, staring into hers.... She bolted upright, slamming her knees into the underside of her desk. She shook her head and blinked to clear her eyes. *I must have drifted off.*

She wiped a strand of drool from her cheek and glanced at her phone. It was 12:14 a.m. A silvery swath of moonlight stretched across her desk to her bed, illuminating the globe that her grandfather had left her when he died. A wisp of moonlight flickered across the surface of the globe as branches outside her window danced in the wind.

Eevie rested her elbows on the desk and cupped her chin in her hands. She felt her mind drifting away again, and somewhere between awake and asleep, a delicate thought kept bubbling to the surface of her consciousness, only to *pop* away when she became slightly aware of it. "Crypticus..."

Eevie shook her head and stared at her globe. "Crypticus," she whispered out loud. *I've never heard of Crypticus.*

She raised the lid of her laptop and typed C-r-y-p-t-i-c-u-s. Google returned 82,000 results. The first result was a death metal band, named Crypticus. *Well, that's not gonna work, unless Grandpa was a head-banger and never told me.*

She changed her strategy and brought up a map of Europe.

She took a look at the globe for reference and then slowly traced her finger down the screen. *There's Italy, Malta...and then the Mediterranean Sea.* She looked at the globe again. *It should be right here.*

She opened a dozen European maps, but Crypticus didn't appear on any of them.

Eevie, fully awake now, looked closer at the strange country. She gently ran her fingers over the surface. Did she feel a small ridge? She placed her nail along the border of Crypticus, and ever so gently pulled. The entire island began to pull away from the globe. She pulled the piece off and began to examine it. She turned it over. She recognized her grandfather's shaky handwriting. It read, *Hide-and-seek > 9th board > knot. I know you will find the answer. Love, Grandpa.*

Eevie's hands shook with excitement. A secret message from her grandpa! She reread the message one more time. She used to love playing hide-and-seek with her grandfather. Her mind immediately filled with images of when she was a little girl hiding from her grandfather. Eevie bolted upright in her chair. She knew exactly where he wanted her to go.

Turning her iPhone to flashlight, she quietly crept through the hallway past her parents' bedroom, down the stairs, to the basement. Slowly, she opened the door at the bottom of the steps. Stale air filled her lungs as she walked into the playroom. The light from her phone danced across a dusty old ping-pong table whose net was now more spider web than net. The light moved over to the giant, rust-colored sectional sofa where she used to hide, and her mind flooded with vivid memories of her grandfather's voice calling and searching for her. Her heart filled with melancholy and excitement simultaneously.

Eevie shone the light on the wall. Strips of stained, knotted pine paneling stretched to the ceiling. She buried her face into the crook of her arm, muffling a sneeze. *This room is in serious need of an extreme makeover...and Febreze.*

Eevie began counting the panels, moving the light from board to board: seven, eight, nine. She stopped at the ninth board. Just above eye level a huge knot beckoned to her. *There it is!* Eevie's heart was pounding. As quietly as she could manage, she pulled part of the sectional sofa away from the wall. A large house spider scurried over her foot. Eevie jumped back, stifling a gasp. *Not cool, Mr. Spider.*

Eevie put her fingers on the knot. Immediately she felt some give, as the top dipped inward. She pressed a little harder and the knot fell into the space behind the board. Standing on her toes, she raised the light and tried to peer down into the hole. Nothing. She slid her fingers into the hole, slowly feeling as she walked her fingers downward.

Eevie's fingers touched something metallic—some sort of latch! She pulled upwards. There was a click, and just like that, the board swung open like a miniature door. Eevie moved the light up and down the length of the opening. At the bottom of the doorway lay a cloth satchel. She crouched down and slowly grabbed the bag. She could tell by its weight that something was definitely inside.

Eevie couldn't stand it. She had to find out what was inside the satchel, but not here. She peered inside the empty doorway. *There it is*, she thought as she picked up the knot that had fallen through and carefully placed it back where it belonged. Then, ever so cautiously, she closed the door. A soft metallic click let her know that it was securely locked into place.

Eevie crept silently back to her room. Her heart beat wildly as if she were auditioning as a drummer in a rock band. Slowly she closed her door and quietly locked it. She lay the satchel on her bed and then listened for a full minute. The only sound she could hear was the wind blowing through the naked branches of the oak tree outside her window.

Eevie flicked on her bedroom light and took a closer look at the satchel. The flap of the satchel was actually closed by two leather straps secured by two brass buckles. Eevie unclasped each buckle and guardedly pulled back the flap. She gingerly lifted the satchel from the bottom and poured the contents onto her bed.

The contents were wrapped in cloth and bound by prickly sisal string. There was a folded piece of paper under the string. Eevie's hands trembled as she carefully removed the paper. Once again, an elixir of sadness and excitement coursed through her body as she saw her grandfather's handwriting.

Eevie, I knew you would solve the puzzle. My heart is filled with so many wonderful memories spent with you. Inside this package you will find everything that you need. I'm sorry I cannot explain more here, in case this package were to fall into the wrong hands. The clues are within, and you will need to use all of the resources available to you to figure them out. Now, I humbly pass on my quest to you. I know you will find a way to put an end to this.

I love you. Grandpa.
P.S. Pam will be there to help guide you.

Eevie shook her head as a tear slowly journeyed down her cheek. "I love you too, Grandpa," she whispered out loud. She read the last line of the letter again. *Grandpa...who is Pam?*

Eevie grabbed scissors from her desk and cut through the cord. *Did he mean Pam from my mom's book club? Because she rides a golf cart to the end of the driveway just to get her mail.*

She opened the cloth, revealing some old newspaper clippings rolled into a tube and held together by two dry-rotted rubber bands. There also was a book with a cracked leather cover that looked to be hundreds of years old. Tiny flecks of gold were all that remained of the letters that had been burned into the cover.

Eevie picked up a circular mechanical device that appeared to be a bronze compass. Eevie wasn't really sure what it was; she had never seen anything like it before. She examined it closely. There were three circles that moved independently of each other. The outer circle had tiny lines and letters engraved all the way around. There was a slightly smaller circle that had two elongated rectangular shapes cut out, and a pentagonal shape cut through the metal. Spread along the surface of the second circle she read aloud: "E-U-I-O-A..." *They're vowels!* she thought excitedly. The center wheel was much smaller. Eevie slowly turned it and rubbed the tip of her index finger over the surface. *Zodiac symbols!* She stared at the smallest wheel. Deeply carved into the surface were eight constellations, each represented by its zodiac symbol.

Excitement coursed like electricity through Eevie's veins. *I should text Tommy!* She glanced at her phone; 12:40 a.m. flashed on the screen. Eevie rested her teeth on her lower lip and exhaled. The excitement was over-whelming her.

Tommy would want me to text him, Eevie smiled to herself. *Wait till Tommy sees this!* Her eyes traveled across the treasure spread across her bed. Eevie grabbed her phone and opened Messenger. A picture of Tommy's smiling face appeared.

What should I say? I don't want to say too much.

She hesitated and then typed, "Tommy, I found something important! Come over as soon as you can. I'll tell you about it in person."

Eevie sat and stared at her phone expectantly. Nothing. She checked her phone's wireless connection. *Come on!* she willed Tommy to respond. In desperation, she Googled "Contact a friend through telepathy". She closed her eyes, envisioning Tommy's eyes flying open, his hand grabbing his phone—reading her message, and then...still nothing...

I've never been so disappointed in pseudoscience in my life.... He must have turned his phone off. I can't really blame him; he's hardly slept at all since the attack. Eevie was suddenly somber, remembering what her friend had been through.

Eevie glanced at the rolled-up newspaper articles. She could look through those with Tommy in the morning. She had one more satchel to open. The material was soft like felt and was pulled closed by a drawstring at the top. As Eevie began to open the satchel, a shock of pain rushed through her right hand. "Ah!" exclaimed

Eevie. She stared down at her finger in horror. The coiled snake ring that had encircled her finger for months began moving. Its rough scales dug into Eevie's flesh. She dropped the bag and sat motionless, staring at her hand. The snake stopped moving.

Eevie's mind filled with the horrific memory of her and Tommy trapped in the deadly labyrinth. She remembered picking up the skeletal hand of someone less fortunate—realizing too late as a screaming Tommy told her to drop it. She watched in horror, unable to move as the serpent ring slithered from the boney hand onto her finger. Its fangs dug into her flesh, the serpent's eyes filling with blood...her blood.

Now, she looked down at the bag on the bed. Her eyes narrowed.... *The snake doesn't like whatever's in that bag...*

Eevie locked her jaw in determination. *It's only a finger!*

In a flash, Eevie grasped the bag from the bottom, flipped it over, and shook. *What the...* Stars of pain exploded behind her eyes as the snake began constricting. Raising its head, it drove its fangs deep into Eevie's finger.

On the bed lay what looked like a wand. The bottom of the wand was grayish white and looked to be made of chunks of bone, and the body, a solid piece of wood, encircled by another thin piece of twisted wood along its entire length. Embedded in the wand were blood-red stones that glistened and sparkled like diamonds. The tip contained a cylindrical, elongated, red stone in the shape of a hexagon. Without thinking, Eevie grabbed the wand.

A wave of white-hot electricity washed over her body, throwing her against the wall. Immediately, the snake twisted and writhed, viciously cutting deeper into Eevie's finger, its red eyes glowing.

Suddenly, the pressure released from Eevie's finger! The snake flung its head backwards, arching upward, expanding its hood. Eevie stared through tear-filled eyes, and as the snake's body convulsed, tiny cracks appeared along the scales of the serpent. A powerful pulsing energy replaced the pain in Eevie's body. Her eyes narrowed and she forcefully whispered the word "*Deleo*!" Immediately, the wand nearly leapt from her hand as a red light exploded from the tip. Eevie gasped. The serpent, which had held her finger captive for months, vaporized into a cloud of silver dust.

Eevie's eyes moved from her finger to the wand and back to her finger. Her body trembled from the adrenaline pumping through her veins. She wiped the tears from her face with her sleeve.

What—just—happened? She stared in disbelief as her bruised and bloody finger healed right before her eyes. *What was the word "Deleo"? What's happening to me?*

Suddenly, there was a knock at Eevie's bedroom door. Eevie spun around in full panic mode, shoving everything under the blankets.

"Eevie, are you OK in there? I heard a loud crash?"

"Everything's fine, Mom. I just got a little chilly and was grabbing a sweatshirt. I tripped over my science book. It's all good. Sorry I woke you up."

"It's OK. Good night, sweetie."

"Night, Mom." Eevie listened as her mom retreated down the hallway.

She pulled back the blankets on her bed. Everything was there except for the wand. *Where did the wand— thwap!* Instantly the wand appeared back in her hand. The end of the wand pulsed red as if in standby mode.

"OK..." Eevie stared at the wand, confused. She tried to put the wand down, but it seemed to be permanently attached to her palm. *OK, this isn't good!*

Eevie grabbed the tip of the wand and yanked and twisted. *Ouch!* It was as if she were grabbing and twisting one of her fingers.

OK, this isn't weird! Eevie stared at the wand that now extended proudly from the palm of her hand. *My life...is ruined. Maybe this book tells me how to get the wand off my hand.* The tip of the wand glowed red when she said the word "wand." *No, no, no.*

Eevie grabbed the leather-bound book. As she slowly flipped through the pages, a scramble of handwritten, nonsensical letters and symbols adorned each page. On some of the pages, someone had meticulously drawn various flowers, berries, and plants.

"It's all in code," she whispered as she shook her head.

Eevie stared at her hand. "Wait, it's gone again!" She shook her hand and checked the blankets. The wand was nowhere to be found. Eevie turned her eyes skyward. *Thank you! I won't have a small sapling growing from my hand anymore.*

Eevie grabbed the satchel and carefully placed all of the items her grandfather had left her inside. *That's everything, except...* She paused mid-thought. *Except for the wand.*

Instantly, the wand appeared in her hand—the tip glowing fiery red as if to say, "I'm ready to cast some spells!"

Eevie stared at her hand. *I go from having a snake embedded in my finger to a tiny redwood growing out the center of my palm. Thank you, Grandpa...*

Eevie placed the satchel inside her backpack. Everything was made more awkward with the wand protruding from her palm.

Ugh, this is horrible. How am I supposed to go to school? Eevie stared at the wand. *I don't need you right now.*

The wand vanished!

Eevie's eyes flew open wide. She whispered the word "wand." The wand instantly appeared, glowing and vibrating. A wave of energy ran down Eevie's arm.

I don't need you right now. The wand didn't go away.

I said, I don't need you right now. The wand seemed to defiantly exclaim, "You don't mean it!" If a wand had arms to cross, it would be crossing them across its chest right now.

Maybe it's not what *I say, but how I say it.*

Eevie tried again. She imagined a movie director, his hands outstretched, pleading from his director chair. "Eevie, darling, say it with—feeling. *Become* the wand..." Eevie nodded, convincing herself to become *one with the wand.* "With feeling. Emphasis on the *feel.*"

Please, I don't need you right now, Eevie pleaded, feeling each word. The wand vanished! "Yes!" she exclaimed.

Relief and exhaustion swept through Eevie's body. She closed the flap on her backpack and climbed into bed. She half-expectantly checked her phone once more to see if Tommy had messaged her. She wasn't surprised that there were no messages.

She lay her head on her pillow and smiled. She couldn't wait to see Tommy's face when she'd tell him about the wand. "No...!" A flash of pulsating red light filled her room. The wand stood proudly on her palm again, as if saying, "I'm ready!" *Oh, darn it, not again!*

Please, I don't need you right now. The wand vanished and Eevie, exhausted, finally drifted off to sleep.

******

Eevie slowly awoke to Sam Smith's soul-crushing song "Stay With Me." It was 6:00 a.m. on Saturday morning. She had forgotten to turn off her school alarm. Her finger stabbed like a hungry bird at her iPhone's screen, frantically trying to find the snooze button before she woke up her parents.

"Ugh," she moaned. "Make it stop!"

Eevie closed her eyes. It seemed like only a few seconds had passed when her phone chimed. Sleepily, Eevie rolled over and grabbed her phone.

Tommy's face smiled back at her. "I'll be there in 30," he texted.

Eevie looked at the time: 6:15 a.m. Her parents would be asleep for another hour or two.

She texted back: "Come to the front door. My parents are asleep, so be quiet. I'll be waiting for you."

Tommy replied, "Of course." He then signed off with the ever-aloof ninja emoji.

******

Snow had begun to fall as Tommy soundlessly climbed the steps to Eevie's house. He reached up to knock on the door, but as his hand traveled through space, Eevie simultaneously opened the door and leaned out, causing Tommy to hit Eevie square in the forehead with his knuckles instead.

"OW! *Really*?" Eevie asked incredulously.

Tommy snorted involuntarily. "You opened the door so fast.... How was I supposed to know you were going to poke your head out?"

"What?"

"You have to admit, that was funny."

"Come in and be quiet," said Eevie, shaking her head in disbelief.

Tommy nodded and quietly followed Eevie to her bedroom.

"Tommy," whispered Eevie as she shut her bedroom door. "Don't say anything, OK? Just listen."

"OK...," said Tommy, barely able to contain his curiosity.

"I found a secret message from my grandfather. He hid it under a fake country on my globe." Eevie showed him the fake country of Crypticus with her grandfather's message written on the back.

"Whoa!" exclaimed Tommy as he turned it over in his hands. "Did you figure out his message?"

"Yes," whispered Eevie. "It wasn't very difficult." She paused for a moment, listening for her parents. "Sorry, I thought I heard something.... Grandpa hid this satchel behind a hollow panel in the old playroom," said Eevie as she pulled the satchel from her backpack.

Tommy's eyes filled with excitement. "Oh cool. What's in it?"

Eevie put her finger to her lips, signaling Tommy to be quiet.

He nodded and mouthed "sorry."

Eevie turned the satchel over and carefully poured the contents onto her bed. Tommy's eyes widened. "What is all of this stuff?" he whispered to Eevie.

"Read this first." She handed Tommy her grandfather's letter.

"It'll help explain things...a little bit."

Eevie separated the items on her bed, while Tommy read the letter.

"Eevie," said Tommy, looking up. "What quest is he talking about?"

"I don't know," said Eevie with a shrug. "I'm sure that the contents of the bag provide some answers, but...my grandfather seems to have written everything in some type of code."

Tommy picked up the cracked, leather-bound book and gently flipped through it. Rows of letters filled the pages, and notes were scribbled on the edges. The handwriting was different from Eevie's grandfather. Circular blotches of ink dotted the pages; the letters looked to have been written with a feather quill, not a pen.

"You're right, it's some sort of code," whispered Tommy as he looked up from the book. "But I don't think your grandfather wrote this. Look at the handwriting on your grandfather's letter, and then look at the writing in this book." Tommy held them side by side. "They're completely different."

Eevie nodded. "I haven't had a chance to try to break the code yet. I just found everything last night. I think it might have something to do with this." Eevie handed Tommy the spherical mechanical tool. "You see how it has letters and marks like a compass or a clock?"

Tommy nodded, studying the device. He rotated the circles slowly, one by one, with his fingers. Something about this device seemed vaguely familiar to him.

"Eevie, each piece moves independently of each other, and there are also zodiac symbols. I bet if we figure out how to use this thing, we'll be able to figure out how to read the book."

"I think so too," whispered Eevie, nodding her head.

"I've got an idea." Tommy pulled out his phone and took a picture of the strange device. He then opened the book once again and took pictures of several pages.

"Next, I'll open Google Image Search, and..."

"Tommy," said Eevie apprehensively. "Before you do that, there's one more thing I need to show you. Promise me you won't freak out."

Tommy was about to make a joke—but there was something in Eevie's eyes that said, "If you value your life, you'll be cool about what I'm going to show you."

Before she could change her mind, Eevie thrust out her hand and whispered, "Wand."

Tommy jumped back. "Whoa, Eevie, what the—?! You...you have a wand growing out of your hand! It's so cool!"

Eevie smacked Tommy on the forehead with the wand. The diamond shone brightly as if asking, "He's annoying. Shall I obliterate him now, Master?"

"Ow, geez!" said Tommy as he rubbed his head. "You get a wand and you have to go all gangster on me?"

"Tommy, you jerk, it's permanently attached to me somehow! If I say the word 'wand' it just appears." The wand hummed and glowed brighter when she said "wand."

"What do you mean...a part of you?" asked Tommy, his eyes narrowing.

"I mean, it's like a part of my body now." She held out her hand. The wand stood proudly on her palm, as if saying, "Please try me—I'm filled with awesome-ness."

"Well, can't you just pull it off? I mean, it's not really connected to anything."

Eevie shook her head. "Trust me, I've tried."

"Well, you didn't have it when I got here, so..."

"I don't need you," said Eevie while staring at the wand.

"That's really harsh.... Oh...wait...you meant the wand. It's gone!" Tommy's eyes traveled from her palm to her face, back to her palm. "We're going to be rich!"

"Eevie?" There was a loud knock on her door.

Eevie's eyes flew open. "Tommy, get out of here!" she whispered.

"Where?" asked Tommy, looking around the room frantically.

"One sec, Mom. Be right there."

Eevie pointed at the window. "There. Go!"

Tommy looked at Eevie as if she had lost her mind. She quickly threw open the window. Tommy climbed over the desk, and he was about to crawl through the first-floor window when he turned to Eevie. "I've had enough of windows!"

Undeterred, Eevie offered her compassion by pushing him out the window, and once again he was falling through space.

In a perfect world, Tommy would have jumped out, tucked and rolled onto the blanket of freshly fallen snow, and then slowly jogged home and slow-roasted his toes by the fireplace. However, ever since Tommy participated in the "Facts and Fiction" challenge at school, in which he debated and argued vehemently that there was no such thing as karma or Murphy's Law, bad things seemed to happen.

And true to form, the lace of Tommy's shoe caught on the window ledge, leaving Tommy, hands buried in the snow, performing an almost perfect handstand outside Eevie's window.

Eevie's mom knocked again. "Eevie!"

"Come to the front door in five minutes!" Eevie whispered urgently.

"Eevie!" Tommy cried out.

Eevie slammed the window down, then heard a muffle cry of "Ouch!" Tommy's foot was trapped in the window.

Eevie's mom knocked again. "EEVIE!"

"Coming, Mom."

In a panic, Eevie quickly slid the globe in front of Tommy's trapped foot, then ran to her bedroom door and flung it open.

"Good morning, Mother," said Eevie, giving her mom her brightest morning smile. Eevie looked like a miniature, younger version of her mother, shoulder-length light brown hair, brown eyes, and a thin, athletic build. At this moment, however, her mother resembled a middle linebacker as she filled Eevie's doorframe.

Mrs. Davenport's eyes roamed suspiciously around her room. "Who were you talking to?" Her questions sounded more like a command than a question.

"I was... I was Skyping with Tommy," said Eevie through a yawn. "He's on his way over."

Outside, Tommy slowly tried to work his foot out of the window. *See*, he told himself, *this isn't Karma, I wanted to practice my handstands and the opportunity presented itself. It had nothing to do with the fact that my best friend just* shoved *me out her window!*

Tommy could hear Eevie and her mom talking. *Oh my God—hello? I'm hanging here by my foot...how hard can it be to get your mom out of your room? Or even better, unhook my shoelace—anything!*

Just then the neighbor's door opened. Mr. Dudley stepped out into the wintry morning, enshrined in what could only be described as a mucous-colored robe that revealed white pasty legs and slippers. He stood regally on his porch, one hand buried in his pocket and the other hand holding a steaming cup of coffee.

"Not fair," whispered Tommy to himself. *Right now, he could pour that coffee all over me and I'd be fine with it...my fingers are turning into popsicles.*

Just when Tommy thought things couldn't get any worse, he watched in horror as Mr. Dudley opened the door again. Champ the Chihuahua strutted out onto the porch in his New England Patriots sweater and booties and pretentiously sniffed the air.

"Go potty!" said Mr. Dudley, gesturing toward the neighbor's yard. Even from his upside-down perch, Tommy could tell that the "neighbor's" yard was Eevie's yard.

I knew it! He's the jerk that's been letting his dog poop on Eevie's grass. That dog is a disgrace to the Patriots's uniform.

There seemed to be no limit as to how many bushes Champ would claim as his domain. If nothing else, Champ had to be admired for his consistency. One by one he marked his territory. If any intruder dared to venture within the bounds of his domain, he or she would face the ferocity of this five-pound warrior who would gallantly defend this row of boxwoods to the death.

Champ was about five bushes in when he froze in his tracks and sniffed the air. Painfully, Tommy rotated his head, and that's when their eyes met. Champ was so close he could smell his breath. It smelled of victory, determination, and old socks. Like all great warriors, Champ seemed to assess the situation, and being an opportunist, determined that Tommy was officially declared boxwood number 6.

Tommy looked pleadingly at Champ, but he could see in the dog's eyes that a decision had been made, and there was no turning back.

"Nice puppy," Tommy whispered nervously. "I'm a Patriots fan too. Go Brady!"

Undeterred, Champ moved forward.

Tommy also was a fighter, and he tried another tactic. Shifting his weight onto his left hand, he attempted to scoop up snow and shoo Champ away, but his left arm was too weak to support him. Tommy clenched his teeth as his chin hit the ground. He struggled to his forearms and with great difficulty raised his head. There stood Champ. They were nose to wet nose, eyeball to tiny eyeball. "You have beautiful eyes," moaned Tommy.

Champ gave Tommy a sniff and then, after much consideration, decided that this strange-looking bush was worthy of being part of his protected turf. Everything seemed to happen in slow motion. Champ's body was turning sideways, his hind leg raising up. Tommy's face scrunched up in anticipation of becoming a part of Champ's territory, while simultaneously smashing his face into the ground. His body followed, crumpling to the ground in an undignified heap.

Like the true warrior that he was, Champ leapt backwards through the air, barking his disapproval. Then, with an unrelenting drive to accomplish the task at hand, he dutifully raised his leg and peed on the butt portion of Tommy's jeans. "I feel so alone," whispered Tommy.

Champ turned and began kicking out his hind legs, covering Tommy in tiny little showers of snow. Satisfied with his conquests, Champ marched back to his owner's house with purpose.

Tommy slowly stood, then leaned against Eevie's house. He was incredibly dizzy, half frozen, and missing one sneaker...at least his butt was warm. Tommy reached up and pulled the lace out of his shoe, then left it hanging on the windowsill. He put his shoe on and hobbled to Eevie's front door.

Tommy was blowing warm air on his hands as Eevie opened the door. "Eevie Davenport, you are a horrible person. You literally shoved me headfirst out a window, into a blizzard. I've had enough bad experiences with windows to last me a lifetime."

Eevie shook her head. "Remind me to craft a papier-mâché Oscar for you. So much drama. You fell three feet!"

"On my head!" Tommy reminded her.

"Oh, I thought you were the guy with catlike reflexes.... That must have been some other genius athlete."

"I didn't fall; I was shoved like a human battering ram through your window. We both know I have catlike reflexes, but my foot got..."

"And what is that smell?" interrupted Eevie as she scrunched up her face. "Did you roll in something? I toss you out my window and in five minutes you come back looking like something from *The Walking Dead*."

"Hey, don't belittle *The Walking Dead*—they won a Golden Globe! And yes, I smell like this because Champ the Chihuahua decided to treat me like a human bush."

"Oh, I'm so sorry!" said Eevie, covering her mouth with her hands. "You can think of some horrific way to get me back later." She straightened his shirt. "But we have to get to my room before my mom starts snooping.... Oh, and I know this will be difficult, but when I talk to my mom just go along with what I say, please."

"Or else you'll shove me out the window again?" said Tommy wryly.

"Don't tempt me," Eevie grinned.

Tommy followed Eevie back to her bedroom. Her mom was standing by the edge of her bed. Spread out on the bed was a series of newspaper articles.

"Eevie, where did you get these?"

Eevie's heart leapt to her throat. She thought her mom had found everything, but all she could see were the articles. She paused before she spoke.

"Grandpa left them for me." Eevie stood silently, waiting for the next question, hoping this would give her enough time to think.

"What do you mean he left them for you? When?"

"I don't know when. I just found them last night. I was going to show them to Tommy—that's what we were Skyping about.... I knew you wouldn't approve."

Mrs. Davenport drew in a sigh. "Where did you find them?" she asked, her tone just a touch softer.

"They were hidden behind a loose board in the old playroom—where Papa and I used to play hide-and-seek."

"But you said your grandfather left them for you," said her mom. She tilted her head, letting Eevie know that she knew there was more to the story.

Eevie walked over to the desk, opened the top drawer, and grabbed the island of Crypticus.

"Grandpa created a fake country and hid it on the globe he gave me. He wrote me a message on the back. See?" Eevie showed her mother the back of the imaginary country.

Eevie's mom read it. She shook her head and whispered, "Dad."

She was quiet for a moment. She looked down at the bed covered in newspaper stories.

"Eevie, do you realize that you and Tommy are lucky to be alive?" asked Mrs. Davenport, emphasizing each word. "The park ranger said that he told you that there was a dangerous sinkhole. He *warned* you that it was dangerous...and then for some reason, that I'll never understand, you snuck over there at nighttime." Eevie's mom looked from Eevie to Tommy and shook her head. "You are lucky that there was an underground cavern that connected to that lake, or you would have died."

She paused. Tommy winced, knowing that she was building momentum. "You've been banned from the park, you had search and rescue teams looking for you, and now...now you are sneaking around again?" She looked from Tommy to Eevie, a mixture of dismay and anger crossing her face.

Tommy started to open his mouth, but he remembered what Eevie had said. He decided to do the bravest thing in the world—look down and suddenly become extremely interested in his feet.

Eevie's mind was racing. She knew she had to be careful. She had to diffuse the situation before her mom went ballistic on them. She swallowed hard, hoping that her strategy would work—and that Tommy would soon be crafting a papier-mâché Oscar for her performance.

"Mom," said Eevie, on the verge of tears, "it's not like that at all. I've told you over and over how sorry I am for what happened. I made—"

"*We* made," said Tommy, his voice barely audible. He couldn't take it anymore, and it wasn't fair for Eevie to take all of the blame.

Eevie started again. "We made a very bad decision, and we learned from our mistakes. I didn't mean to find the fake country. It just happened. It's just...when I saw that Grandpa had left me a riddle, I felt...well, it felt like I was playing hide-and-seek again, just this time I wasn't the one hiding.... I Skyped Tommy to see if he could help me figure out the message Grandpa had left me. I knew you and Dad wouldn't be happy, so we figured we would search while you guys were asleep. I'm sorry." Eevie lowered her head and looked at her feet.

Tommy watched as Mrs. Davenport's face softened. He slowly let out his breath—he hadn't realized he'd been holding it in.

As he glanced at the articles spread out over Eevie's blanket, something caught his eye. What was it? He stealthily took a small step to the right. The article closest to him was dated October 17, 1862. The headline read, "George Whitcomb and Darla Rogers Missing at Black Hallow Park." Under the headline were pictures of the two children, and below that picture was a photo of a park ranger named Andrew Miller. Tommy shook his head. A blurb beside the ranger's picture quoted the ranger: "I am using all of the resources available to my team to find the missing children." The thing that shocked Tommy was that...the park ranger was...the same ranger from Black Hallow Park, meaning he would be over 170 years old!

Tommy's heartbeat quickened. He could hear Eevie and her mom's voices tapping at his eardrums, but his eyes were quickly scanning the other articles: one from 1929, more children missing, a picture of a group of men. But the one that stood out was of a bearded ranger named Henry Adams. However, Andrew Miller and Henry were the same person!

Several more articles lay scattered on Eevie's bed, dated 1946, 1965, 2007. The same face, the same evil monster, the same eyes that had been in his house just a few nights ago stared back at Tommy.

Tommy shook his head, trying to wrap his brain around what he was seeing. Slowly, he became aware again of the conversation between Eevie and her mom.

"Eevie, your grandfather meant well, but he could never settle for a normal life. He filled notebook after notebook with stories about ships lost at sea, filled with treasure; undiscovered tombs of Egyptian pharaohs; the Bermuda Triangle.... When I was a little girl he filled my head with fantastic stories. He said one day *he* would be the one finding the treasures, but...they were only just that, Eevie—stories."

Eevie could hear the sadness in her mom's voice. It was the voice of someone who felt like something irreplaceable had been taken from her. Eevie wanted to tell her mom that her dad had truly been on an amazing quest...that magic did exist—she just couldn't. *Maybe someday, she'll see how great of an adventurer her father truly was.*

"Eevie, these disappearances at the park were trage- dies, yes, but they were not because of some magical curse, or whatever fantastical story your grandfather told you. They were accidents, like what happened to you and Tommy, nothing more."

"I know," said Eevie, gently smiling at her mother. "It just seemed so exciting, and I loved Grandpa's sto- ries. He seemed so happy, so alive when he told them." Eevie paused as the words "I miss him" caught in her throat.

"I do too," smiled Eevie's mom, grabbing Eevie in her arms. "I do too."

Eevie's mom hesitated and then carefully collected the newspaper articles from Eevie's bed.

Everyone relaxed. The tension had been diffused— for now. A flash of orange light illuminated Eevie's room as a snowplow rumbled down the street.

"What is that smell?" said Eevie's mom. "It's making my eyes burn."

"And that's my cue," said Tommy as he backed to- ward Eevie's bedroom door. "Eevie, I'll call you later. I better get home before the storm gets too bad. Bye, Mrs. Davenport!"

"Bye, Tommy," she replied, looking somewhat confused by his abrupt departure.

Eevie walked with Tommy to the front door and smiled mischievously. "Be sure to say hi to Champ for me. And oh, stay away from the yellow snow."

Tommy paused and pulled out his soggy wallet. He handed Eevie a ten-dollar bill. "Here, take this. You need it more than me."

Eevie tilted her head, confused. "Why do I need this?"

"Put this toward your college tuition, because you will never make it as a comedian," smiled Tommy. He performed the infamous "mic drop" and then turned and walked out the door.

4

Genius Alert—Inform the Media

Tommy shut his bedroom door. His eyes flicked over to the nightstand, where a small, discolored ring was all that was left where his lamp had once stood. His eyes traveled to his window. Icy-cold fingers raced up his spine, causing him to shiver. He tried, but he couldn't help himself—he checked under his bed and opened his closet. He jabbed his fingers between hanging clothes...he let go a sigh of relief. He was alone.

Tommy sat on his bed, opened his laptop, and connected to his Google cloud account. He navigated to the pictures he had taken at Eevie's. He stopped on the strange circular mechanism. *There you are.* Next, he launched Google Images and uploaded the picture. Within seconds Google returned over 12,000 results.

Tommy stared at the screen. *It's an astrolabe...that was easy.* Tommy read the snippet of text below the image. *Evidence suggests that the astrolabe was in use by ancient astronomers more than 2,000 years ago. The astrolabe was an astronomical computer used for navigation by aligning the rotating spheres with the sun*

and stars. This ingenious device was used for naviga-
tion, determining the position of planets and stars and
finding latitude and longitude.

The next image showed a man standing on the deck
of a ship, his arms outstretched, holding the astrolabe
up to the nighttime sky. A cluster of stars shone through
the three openings in the astrolabe. Tommy recognized
two of the constellations. Small alignment arrows
pointed to numbers on the outer edge of the circle as
well as the innermost circle. The outer circle was very
similar to the photograph that Tommy had taken at
Eevie's, except that there were numbers instead of letters.

Tommy opened the photo of Eevie's astrolabe and
smiled. He was one step closer to breaking the code!

Outside, the wind had picked up and snow was definitely falling harder than before. Disappointed, Tommy
opened his weather app, expecting bad news. However,
it looked like the storm would move out by late after-
noon and the sky would be clear that night. *Finally,*
some good news! Tommy fired off a text to Eevie.

"Genius Alert. I'm pretty sure I've figured out how
to break the code. You can sing my praises later. Give
me a call after you check out the link and the image.
This concludes the Genius Alert."

Seconds later, Tommy's phone vibrated. Eevie replied by texting, "Awesome, I'll call in just a second"
and a thumbs-up emoji, immediately followed by "He

misses you..." with a sad-face emoji and a picture of Champ.

Tommy looked at his phone bewildered. *Oh my God, who is this person who's replaced my best friend? She's always been the sensible one. Well, I'll take the high road and let her have her fun.* Seconds later Tommy replied, "We'll see who's laughing when he takes you to homecoming. I hear he's a great dancer." Followed once again with the mic-drop emoji.

Tommy opened the pictures that he had taken of the old book and printed them. He stared at the images. Soon, he hoped, the jumble of letters would make sense.

Eevie called a few moments later. Tommy could hear the excitement in her voice. "If we need to see the constellations," she effused, "we need to find a place where there isn't much light, so we can see the stars clearly."

"What about the football field? It's only lit up if there's a game...or...," he paused, "*homecoming....* Your date Champ told me that's your special night."

Eevie ignored the last comment and continued Tommy's train of thought.

"It gets dark around 5:30. Let's walk over then."

"OK," said Tommy. "I'll just tell my parents we're going for a walk."

"All right. I'll see you at..."

"Wait," said Tommy, cutting her off. "There's one more thing. You know the newspaper articles that your mom took?"

"Yeah," said Eevie, pausing, waiting for more.

"They were dated from the late 1800s until...well, until now. You know, like present time."

"Yeah," acknowledged Eevie. "Some of them looked pretty old."

"That's just the thing: Every article was about missing children near Black Hallow Park. But the creepiest thing is, each article had a picture of the park ranger."

"OK...," said Eevie, waiting. "That's because it happened at the park."

"No, Eevie, *the* park ranger," said Tommy. "Not different rangers. The same park ranger who tried to...," Tommy paused for a second, "...kill me."

Tommy suddenly became very serious. "The same face, the same eyes—the same person. He had different names, but it was the same person." For the second time that day, an icy chill traveled like electricity up Tommy's spine, causing him to spin around in his chair and look behind him.

"Are you sure? How could it be the same ranger? He'd be over a hundred years old."

"Are you seriously asking me that? Think about it. We escaped from a tree that tried to crush us, and then a crazed, demonic creature whose best friend was some hybrid howler monkey with ginormous fangs tried to kill us. And you're asking me if this could be the same ranger? You have a wand growing out of your hand...which is wicked cool by the way...so yes, the same ranger."

"Well, when you put it that way...," Eevie realized.

"It all seems so *anticlimactic* now," said Tommy dryly.

"We already know the ranger isn't human, but we also have no idea why he is here. All we know is we entered his world, our parents don't believe the world exists, and he—"

"He wants to kill us...so we don't expose his world," added Tommy.

"And there's that...," nodded Eevie.

"Can't we pull up the archives in the library? Don't they have old newspapers at the library or online? Your grandfather left you those articles for a reason. We've just got to figure out how all of this ties together."

"If we get caught looking up Black Hallow stuff in the library, our parents are going to lock us in our rooms and throw away the keys."

"What about Drew? We know he can be trusted. He can search the archives at the library and download the images. I'll shoot him a text and see if he wants to go with us to the football stadium. We can fill him in there."

"OK," said Eevie. "Sounds great. See you at 5:30."

Eevie pulled out the astrolabe and the mysterious book from her backpack and laid them on her desk. She removed the astrolabe from its protective satchel and held it toward her ceiling, imagining stars shining through the openings. "Grandpa," she said smiling and turning the astrolabe over in her hand, "I think we're one step closer to figuring out your puzzle."

5

STARLIGHT, STAR BRIGHT, FIRST STAR

I SEE TONIGHT

White skeletal branches stretched skyward, silhouetted against the nighttime sky. Stars sprinkled like glitter across the heavens. They shimmered as if they too were excited about the secret they were about to reveal. Below, a ferocious wind ripped across the parking lot, creating cyclones of snow and ice.

A lone figure crouched in the shadowed doorway of the stadium. The rope connected to the flagpole clanged noisily with every gust of wind.

"Drew," called out Tommy. "Is that you?"

"Hey, guys," said Drew through chattering teeth. "Why all the secrecy?"

"Drew, we need your help..."

"Wait a minute," said Drew, raising his gloved hands. "I almost got you guys killed.... I'm not getting involved in anything crazy again."

"Are those pink Hello Kitty gloves?" asked Tommy as he leaned in for a closer look.

Drew thrust his hands back into his puffy blue winter coat. "They're my sister's," he said defensively. "I couldn't find mine."

And oddly they fit you.... "OK," mouthed Tommy, smiling.

"Drew," said Eevie, putting her hand on his shoulder. "What happened to me and Tommy was our decision, our fault. We could really use your help with this."

"Yeah," said Tommy, his teeth chattering. "Just because you decided to tell a fantastical story about a demon-possessed tree almost killing you—and then getting Eevie and I nearly killed—we still…"

"We still value your friendship," smiled Eevie.

Drew stared into Eevie's eyes. Warmth filled his body. Romantic music filled his soul. He was pretty sure that his heart was now pumping tiny heart-shaped cells throughout his body. All he needed now was Cupid to appear and fulfill his prophecy. "I'm yours," whispered Drew as if in a trance.

"What?" asked Eevie, shaking her head.

"Plus," interrupted Tommy, "it's already begun again," he said, unaware of Drew's awkward profession of love.

"Wait.... Wha-what's begun again?" stammered Drew, this time not from the cold.

"The break-in at my house. It wasn't a burglar—it was the ranger. He tried to kill me!"

Drew's mouth flew open, but no words came out. *Sorry, Eevie, yet again our love will have to wait for the betterment of humanity.*

"Drew, we're not here to do anything crazy. Relax," said Eevie calmly. "Remember when I told you the story about my grandfather and how he found pictures and newspaper clippings hidden in his father's office?"

"Yes," said Drew tentatively. "The story of the shoe-horn."

Tommy snickered. "Shoehorn."

Eevie continued, ignoring the two boys. "Well, my grandfather left me a hidden message, and when I solved the message, I found a bunch of strange items that he had left for me."

"Why didn't he just give them to you?" asked Drew.

"Drew, he didn't want anyone to know what he was up to. Think about when you told people about the tree, how they reacted. No one believed you. Just as no one believes me and Tommy... My parents blamed my grandfather for filling my head with crazy stories, even though I think my grandfather was the most amazing man I've ever known. I think that he did things the way he did them because he wanted me to be ready."

Drew's round face paled with uncertainty. "Eevie, what the heck did you find?"

Eevie pointed to her backpack. "It's all in here. Let's get into the stadium, and out of this wind, and I'll show you."

The trio traversed the icy sidewalk to the front of the stadium. Eevie and Tommy were extremely familiar with Swift Creek Middle School's pride and joy, the Northwood Sports Complex.

Tommy played football and track here, and Eevie played soccer. Drew was familiar with another part of the stadium...the bleachers. Tommy walked up to the main gate and gave his friends the thumbs down gesture. There was no way they were getting in through the gates. A huge chain and padlock the size of New Hampshire made sure no one was getting in without a key...a really big key.

"Worth a try," smiled Tommy. "Drew, I hope you're not afraid of heights," he said, looking up at the ten-foot chain-link fence that surrounded the stadium.

Eevie looked at Drew apprehensively. She was about to ask if he was cool with climbing it. As if reading her mind, Drew attacked the fence and began ascending. He turned to Tommy and yelled out, "You coming?"

Eevie laughed at Tommy. Even in the darkness, she could see Tommy's face redden. "Come on, Champ," she said, punching him in the shoulder.

"Champ.... I get it.... Funny."

Clambering over the fence in gloves and boots while pummeled by thirty-miles-per-hour winds was not the easiest or most enjoyable thing in the world. However, Drew seemed to have watched every single episode of *American Ninja Warrior* as he leapt off the fence from about ten feet up, landing a perfect snow belly flop.

Tommy cringed. He heard and felt the impact as Drew slammed into the snow. He expected Drew to sit up and half of his teeth would be missing. However, Drew flipped over and stared into Eevie's eyes while making a perfect snow angel. He then sat up and drew little hearts at the tip of each wing.

"Whoa, cool," said Eevie, laughing at Drew. "That was awesome!"

Tommy clung to the top of the fence and shook his head. No way Drew Morris was gonna steal his thunder. This was the kid who normally tripped over his own shadow. Without looking, Tommy leapt into the air. *Oh no*, was the only thought that entered Tommy's head as his body smashed into the ground.

Tommy rolled over, gasping for air. As he slowly sat up, he looked like someone had hit him in the face with a snow pie.

"You OK?" asked Eevie, trying not to laugh.

"You OK, bud?" asked Drew, a little too smugly. Tommy could see a little glistening of happiness in Drew's eyes.

"I'm fine, I'm fine—I just landed wrong. Come on," said Tommy, getting to his feet, "let's go to the concession stand and get out of this wind." Suddenly, Tommy was blinded by a flash of light.

"What the...?"

"Sorry," laughed Drew, holding up his phone. "I had to get a picture of you with the snow beard. You know you look a lot like a young Colonel Sanders."

"Seriously?" asked Tommy. "Unbelievable."

"Um, I'll delete it," said Drew, seeing the look of impending doom in Tommy's eyes.

Eevie smiled and playfully brushed the snow beard from Tommy's face. "Come on, guys. Let's concentrate on what we came here for."

Eevie, Tommy, and Drew huddled under the shelter of the concession stand. Eevie cleaned the snow away, placed her backpack on the counter, and unzipped it.

"Eevie," said Tommy as she began removing the items from the backpack. "Do you think that Drew should read the letter your grandfather wrote you first? It kind of puts things in context."

"Yeah, good idea," nodded Eevie.

She handed the note to Drew, while Tommy watched Drew's expressions.

"Eevie, watch. Drew moves his lips when he reads," whispered Tommy just loud enough for Drew to hear.

Eevie gave Tommy the *seriously* look that every girl has mastered when they feel the need to make their male friend aware that they are being trifling.

"So...," said Drew, pausing, "your grandfather is asking you to solve some riddles, so you can take over his quest? Not trying to be rude, but from what I've seen and read, *quests...*," he fought back the impulse to do air quotes, "...by their very nature don't tend to be safe."

"Yes, I know. I guess I'm just gonna have to trust that my grandfather saw something in me, or knows something that I don't know. Look, he also knew that I have the best friends in the world, and that they *always* have my back." She paused and smiled at each of them. "Let's at least see if we can figure out my grandfather's clues and find out where it takes us."

"I'm in," said Drew, smiling. "I'll help however I can."

Eevie looked at Tommy, her eyebrows raised questioningly.

"I don't know. It sounds dangerous. Maybe you should ask Champ. I'm sure he'd volunteer to take my place."

"Champ?" inquired Drew, jealousy creeping in.

"Champ is Eevie's new boyfriend. He's taking her to homecoming."

"Boyfriend," whispered Drew, crestfallen. It was as if Cupid had drawn back his bow only to have the string snap right when he was about to let his arrow of love fly.

Tommy couldn't take it. Drew's mournful expression was heart-wrenching. "Yeah, Eevie and Champ are pretty close," he teased. "Oh, here's a picture of Champ," said Tommy, holding out his iPhone.

"Champ's a dog...?" asked Drew, confused and relieved.

"Woah, that's harsh. I mean I agree he's no Chris Hemsworth, but as they say, love is blind," laughed Tommy.

"Drew, I am not going to homecoming with Champ. However...I may or may not have a poster of Chris Hemsworth in his Thor costume on my wall..."

"Or two," interjected Tommy.

"Or two," added Eevie, "but for now, can we please remember why we are here?"

"Sorry, Eevie," smiled Drew meekly.

Eevie gave Tommy the stink-eye, followed by the infamous two-finger *I'm watching you* exchange.

Eevie pulled out the cloth satchel from her backpack. The concession stand shook and groaned with each gust of wind. The first item she removed was the instrument that Tommy had identified as an astrolabe.

"It's an astrolabe," said Tommy, seeing Drew's puzzled expression. "Explorers used it for navigation. You see the holes?" He turned the astrolabe toward Drew. "We think that if we align it with the stars correctly it will help us solve the code."

Eevie slowly unwrapped the cloth protective covering from the ancient book, and then placed the book on the counter. "Here's the book my grandfather left me."

Drew gently opened the cover. "Your grandfather wrote this?" asked a confused Drew. "Because..."

"I know, because it's written with a quill or a nib," said Eevie, "and not an ink pen. I don't think my grandfather wrote this. I think it was given to him, or he found it. We're not sure how old it is, but we hope to find out once we decipher the code."

"Which we better do quickly," said Tommy, "before our parents begin getting worried. I'd like to stay off their radar as long as possible."

Eevie, Tommy, and Drew trudged through the snow to the middle of the stadium, as ice crystals glistened like diamonds beneath the moonlight. The night sky was perfectly clear.

"OK, Eevie," Tommy said, "according to what I read, we are supposed to align the holes in the middle circle with three groups of stars. The inner circle should then be rotated to match the zodiac representation of the constellation that appears in the hole."

"Wow, Tommy," said Eevie, through chattering teeth, "I'm impressed."

"Thank you, Eevie, as you should be. Drew," said Tommy, smiling, "you need to step up your game." Tommy expected Drew to have some type of retort. However, he was concentrating on whatever he was doing on his phone.

"If you pull out a selfie stick, I'm going to vomit," said Tommy.

"OK," said Eevie, staring at the sky, "it looks absolutely chaotic up there. Beautiful, but chaotic. How am

I supposed to know which zodiac symbol matches the constellation? Or, how to even find a constellation...?"

"I just downloaded the Star Chart app," said Drew smugly. "I figured instead of standing here all night aimlessly pointing that thing at the sky, I thought I'd use this app to identify the constellations. Then we can use the astrolabe and see if any of them align in the openings."

"Dang, looks like someone brought their 'A' game, Tommy," Eevie said.

"Actually, that was a good idea," said Tommy, surprised at Drew's ingenuity. "I take back everything I ever said about you."

"All right, Drew, you're up!" said Eevie.

Drew held his phone to the sky. His phone's screen jumped to life, analyzing and separating stars into grids. His phone locked onto a series of stars and drew a line connecting them. "It found Gemini," said Drew excitedly.

Tommy looked at Drew's screen, and then at the sky. "I would never have found that without those lines connecting the stars."

Eevie held the astrolabe up to the sky. She rotated the circle with the holes in it until she could see Gemini through the hole. "OK, I have Gemini lined up. Is there another constellation close to Gemini? It would have to be to the right of Gemini."

Drew held his phone to the sky. A few moments later his phone locked onto another cluster of stars.

"Got it. It looks like something called Auriga, and...it seems to be connected to Taurus."

Drew held his phone up beside the astrolabe so Eevie could align it into the correct position. She tried to align the stars, but they did not line up with the holes.

"Am I looking at the right set of stars?" she asked. "It's not lining up at all, no matter how I twist this thing."

"Eevie, what if Gemini is supposed to be in the right hole, and the other constellation should be to the left?" asked Tommy. He turned to Drew. "Is there another constellation to the left of the astrolabe?"

Drew slowly panned his phone to the left. Stars and grids intersected and then a pattern began to emerge.

"Cancer!" said Drew excitedly. "Eevie, it's almost directly across from Gemini." Drew held his phone to the left of the astrolabe so Eevie could see.

Eevie rotated the circle with the holes, and then stopped. She could now see Cancer and Gemini in the opening. Two brilliant stars appeared in the third smallest window.

"It lines up!" shouted Eevie. "Drew," said Eevie excitedly, "can you point your app at these two stars?" She pointed to the stars beaming through the third hole.

"Don't point your phone at me, Drew, unless you want to see the Hercules constellation," said Tommy as he arched his eyebrows upward.

Drew aligned his phone directly under the astrolabe. "It's a constellation called Canis Minor; it's right under Gemini. The app says it means 'lesser dog.' I think that would be more befitting of Tommy..."

"Hey, wait, so it's a legit constellation then?" said Tommy excitedly.

"Yes," said Eevie, "and everything lines up!"

"Don't move a thing on the astrolabe!" said Tommy. "I'm going to take a picture of it." Tommy's phone flashed. "In fact, I'm going to take a *few* pictures just in case they aren't perfectly clear."

"Guys, I'm thinking—Eevie you probably don't want to leave the astrolabe where it's showing the answer. You know, in case someone were to find it."

Eevie paused, turning to Drew. "That's a good idea."

"Tommy's got pictures now. Why not upload them to a password-protected folder that we can all access? We can figure out the code from the pictures."

Tommy nodded. "I'll get them uploaded as soon as I get home." He turned to Eevie. "In the meantime, I would hide the astrolabe someplace separate from the book. That way they are never together."

"Will do," smiled Eevie. "I know just the place. For now, I'll keep the book hidden, and I'll put another book cover over it, so it looks like a different book."

Drew's phone beeped, and the screen flashed 7:00. "FYI, I only have until about 8:30," said Drew, looking up.

"Then we better get moving!" said Tommy.

The three friends raced to the concession stand. Eevie's backpack had blown over. The book was teetering on the edge of the counter, the pages flipping wildly in the wind.

"Ugh," said Eevie, "that wasn't bright."

"It's OK," said Drew. "We were all excited, and the book is fine."

Eevie went to wrap the book, but the covering was nowhere to be found. She checked in and under her backpack, but it wasn't anywhere.

"What's wrong, Eevie?"

"The covering for the book, it's gone. It must have blown away."

"In this wind, you'll never find it," said Tommy. "It was just a covering, right?"

"Yeah, I guess..." Inside, Eevie struggled with losing anything that belonged to her grandfather. It was like losing yet another part of their connection.

The three looked for another couple minutes and then agreed that they needed to go.

Tommy knew Eevie better than anyone else in the world. He could see the sadness flash in her eyes. "Don't worry," said Tommy, putting his arm around

Eevie. "I have a feeling that we are going to learn a lot more about your grandfather."

It was a tender moment that had to be interrupted by Drew.... He handed the cover to Eevie, "The wind blew it against the fence. It's soaking wet, but I'm sure it will dry."

Eevie grabbed the cloth as if she were starving and it was the last scrap of food on the plate. "You found it! Thank you so much!"

"OK, OK," said Tommy, slightly annoyed. "Let's go!"

The three trekked to Tommy's house, each barely able to contain the excitement of finding out what was hidden in the mysterious book.

6

EEVIE HAS A BRIGHT IDEA

After exchanging brief hellos with Tommy's parents, the group escaped upstairs to his bedroom. "OK," said Tommy, closing the door and smiling, "we've got a code to break!"

"I'll grab the astrolabe," said Eevie while taking off her backpack. "I haven't changed the positioning yet."

Eevie pulled the astrolabe out of her backpack and shook her head. "I hope this thing is rustproof. If not, I've probably just destroyed a thousand years of history by wrapping it in this soaking wet cloth."

"Egad, Pam would be mortified," said Tommy, smiling.

Eevie placed the wet cloth on the radiator to dry beside a pair of Tommy's socks.

"May I see it?" asked Drew while reaching for the astrolabe. "It looks like it was made from brass," he said as he turned it over in his hands, "so it should be fine. Brass doesn't rust. Only iron-bearing materials rust, so it should be fine."

"Iron Man's nemesis, the common garden hose...," laughed Tommy.

"I don't think Iron Man's suit is actually made out of iron. I believe it's made of Nitinol, a nickel-titanium alloy," said Drew, shaking his head in disapproval.

"Eevie," said Tommy, smiling, "I think you're safe—it appears that Drew is officially dating Wikipedia."

"OK, guys," she replied with a sigh, "we don't have a lot of time. Let's try to break this code and figure out what the other symbols mean."

Tommy grabbed his laptop and the group settled together on the cool wooden floor.

"I think we should start with the letters on the outer circle, just as they are presented on the astrolabe," said Drew. "They are etched into the metal, so we know that they can't change."

"I agree," nodded Eevie, holding the astrolabe out so everyone could see. "Should we start with T? It's the first letter after the word *apex*?"

"I think so," said Tommy as he opened a text document on his laptop. "It's not like we have a starting point."

Eevie began to read the letters out loud—"T-D-E-W-G-V-B-J-K..."—as Tommy's fingers flew across the keyboard.

"Wait!" said Drew, startling his companions. "Eevie, may I see the astrolabe?"

"Sure," said Eevie, handing it to Drew.

Drew placed the astrolabe on the floor, pulled out his phone, and opened the camera app. Leaning over the astrolabe, he expanded the resolution to 3X magnification. The edge of the outer circle filled his screen.

"Look!" he said excitedly. "Eevie, you know how you rotated the second wheel to align the openings with the constellations? Well, there's a small arrow beside the hole you lined up with the Cancer constellation."

"The arrow has a tiny letter A engraved into it. It points right at P—the P on the outer circle. Look!"

Eevie leaned forward and, sure enough, she could see the arrow with a tiny letter A etched into the tip of the arrow.

"I see it!" whispered Eevie excitedly.

"So wait," said Tommy, "before we give Drew the Genius of the Day lapel pin, let's type out the letters starting at the A and then try aligning them with the astrolabe."

"Then we can try a sentence from the book to see if it works," interjected Eevie.

Tommy quickly typed out the alphabet into two rows.

"OK, Eevie, I'm starting with the letter A, and if Drew is correct, then you should start with the letter P and then call out the letters clockwise."

"Got it." Eevie nodded and began calling out the letters.

A	B	C	D	E	F	G
P	*R*	*H*	*U*	*M*	*O*	*T*

H	I	J	K	L	M	N
D	*E*	*W*	*G*	*V*	*B*	*J*

O	P	Q	R	S	T	U
K	*S*	*Y*	*L*	*X*	*F*	*Z*

V	W	X	Y	Z
A	*I*	*N*	*Q*	*C*

Tommy leaned back from his laptop. "All right, Eevie," he said excitedly, "grab the book!"

Eevie quickly jumped up and grabbed the book from her backpack and opened it to the first page. The penmanship was immaculate. Eevie's voice trembled with excitement as she read the first row of letters to Tommy.

"H-L-M-P-F-M-X, space, P-J, space, K-L-R, space, K-O, space, V-E-T-D-F."

"OK, give me just a second to match up the letters," said Tommy excitedly. "It's working! It's working! The first word is C-r-e-a-t-e-s!"

"Awesome!" whispered Eevie, jumping to her feet. She could barely contain herself.

"Next is a-n," Tommy paused. "And then...o-r-b o-f l-i-g-h-t!"

"Woah!" said Drew, looking from Eevie to Tommy. "It actually worked. Creates an orb of light! What does that even mean?" he asked, not really expecting an answer.

"Try the next line," urged Eevie eagerly.

"OK, what's the next set of letters?"

"E-J-H-P-J-F-P-F-E-K-J, space, V-Z-H-E-X, space, K-L-R-M-B."

"OK, give me just a second."

The seconds seemed to take an eternity as Tommy mouthed out each letter.

"I-n-c-a-n-t-a-t-i-o-n..." Tommy paused. "I'm not sure if this is right. It spells L-u-c-i-s O-r-b-e-m? Sounds like an accountant with really bad hair."

"*Lucis Orbem* must be some kind of spell, because it says *incantation*," said Drew.

"*Lucis Orbem* sounds Latin," said Eevie.

Tommy opened Google and clicked Google Translate, and then opened the Latin tab.

"*Lucis* means Light...and *Orbem* means..."

"*Orbem*. *Orbem* means Orb," said Eevie hurriedly. "So, the first sentence describes the spell and the second sentence is the actual spell!"

Tommy's eyes met Eevie's; he knew what she was thinking. She gave him a tiny nod.

"Let's finish deciphering this page, before we do anything else," said Eevie.

Drew looked at Eevie and Tommy, confused for a moment, but then nodded his head in agreement. *They must know something that I don't know.*

Eevie began reading the letters again. Tommy was already deciphering the code as she was reading aloud.

"F-K, space, M-N-F-E-J-T-Z-E-P-D, space, F-D-M, space, V-E-T-D-F."

"T-o e-x-t-i-n-g-u-i-s-h t-h-e l-i-g-h-t," breathed Tommy.

"If it follows the same pattern, the next line will be the spell," said Eevie.

Eevie read out the final letters on the page.

"E-J-H-P-J-F-P-F-E-K-J, space, M-N-F-E-J-H-F-E-B, space, K-L-R-M-B."

A moment later, Tommy read out, "Incantation...*Extinctim Orbem!*"

"It's the same pattern," said Drew. "Incantation, which means *a spell*, and *Extinctim Orbem*...my guess is, it makes the light go out? Like extinct or extinguish?"

"Yep, you're exactly right," said Tommy as he looked at Google Translate. "Once again Drew has confirmed he's in an exclusive relationship with Wikipedia. My condolences, Eevie."

"Wait, wait, wait," said Drew, undeterred by Tommy's jabs. "You just said the *spell* a minute ago and nothing happened. See: *Lucis Orbem! Lucis*

Orbem! *Extinctim Orbem*! See, nothing." Drew's face was filled with disappointment.

"What he doesn't see," said Tommy, "is some poor guy sitting in his kitchen in Kentucky, complaining that his lights keep going on and off."

"Oh my God," Eevie snorted at Tommy's joke.

"Well, what good are spells if they don't work? There's nothing else on the page explaining what to do, and we have no idea *what* illuminates."

"I think that I might have an idea," said Eevie, smiling mischievously at Drew. "Tommy," said Eevie as she turned to face him, "lock your door."

Drew looked from Eevie to Tommy and back to Eevie. "Uhm, guys...," said Drew hesitantly, "you're acting a little weird."

"You'll be fine," said Tommy, placing his hand on Drew's shoulder.

"Seriously," said Drew, looking from Eevie to Tommy. "What's going on?"

"Drew, relax," said Eevie reassuringly. "Listen, my grandfather left behind one more thing that we—well I—haven't shown you yet. You just have to promise me that you *will not* freak out," said Eevie. She turned serious. "Drew, for real...?"

"I promise," said Drew hesitantly.

Eevie stretched out her arm and turned her palm toward the sky. She whispered the word "wand."

Instantly the wand appeared in the center of her hand. The red diamond tip pulsed.

Drew immediately screamed in a high falsetto and threw himself backwards into Tommy's bookshelf, burying himself in an avalanche of books and papers.

OK, that's what Tommy wished had happened. Instead, Drew's head shot back, and then he exclaimed, "Awesome, Eevie! Your grandfather gave you a wand, an actual magic wand," Drew said. "*That* is so cool! Now I understand!"

The wand seemed to vibrate happily as if to say, "I like this human. Can we keep him?"

"OK, OK," said Tommy, looking bewildered. "What has happened to you two? Who has taken over my friends' bodies and when are they coming back?"

The wand vibrated again as if to say, "Hey, I don't think the other guy was finished praising me. Please let him continue."

"Let's try the spells!" Drew exclaimed eagerly.

Eevie nodded, and her hand closed tightly around her wand. "*Lucis Orbem!*"

Immediately a brilliant ball of white light emanated from the tip of the wand.

"It worked," whispered Tommy, stunned.

Eevie wasn't sure how or why she knew to do this, but she flicked her wrist and the ball of light flew to the corner of Tommy's room, attaching itself and illuminating everything around it.

She flicked her wand back toward her and immediately the light flew back to the wand.

"How did you do that?" whispered Drew in amazement.

"I'm not sure," replied Eevie. "It just felt...right."

Eevie flicked her wrist again toward Tommy's window. The ball of light flashed across the room and smooshed out like a radiant raindrop bathing the surface of the window and floor in light.

"*Extinctim Orbem*," Eevie whispered. The expansive ball of light constricted and flew back to Eevie's wand—and vanished.

"I don't need you," spoke Eevie softly. The wand vibrated and then disappeared into the palm of her hand.

Everyone stood in rapt silence absorbing what had just happened. They had solved the first clue...but they still had no idea what Quest they were supposed to undertake.

The silence was broken by two soft chimes. Drew jumped and grabbed at his pocket. "It's 8:15, guys. I gotta get home."

Tommy nodded. "Eevie, can you leave the astrolabe with me tonight? I want to see if I can figure out what the other symbols mean. I'll Skype you and Drew the code, so we each have a copy."

"Sure," said Eevie as she put on her coat and gloves. Tommy's eyes traveled to his window, where just a moment earlier the sticky white glow of light had filled his eyes. Just below the ledge of his window, three shallow black grooves were a constant reminder of his brutal attack. The monster's blood had seared the wood like drops of acid. Tommy shuddered. He wouldn't dare divulge to his friends how many nights he had awoken in a cold sweat—gasping for air.

"Tommy? Tommy, you OK?" Eevie was touching his shoulder.

"Yeah, I'm fine," said Tommy, nodding. "I was just thinking about the clues. Sorry."

The group walked down the stairs to the front door in silence.

"Mom, Dad, I'm walking Eevie home. I'll be right back," shouted Tommy.

"OK," said Tommy's mom. "Come straight back."

"I will," said Tommy, closing the door.

The moon shone down on the trio, casting long, inky shadows over the snow. Skeletal trees stretched skyward like bony fingers reaching for the stars.

"I'm going to try to decipher more of the book tonight," said Eevie, already envisioning herself decoding page after page. Eevie turned to Drew. "If you want, I'll take some pictures of some of the pages and text them to you, so you can help decode the book too."

"OK, cool," said Drew enthusiastically. "I can't wait!"

They reached the corner of Cottonwood Avenue. Drew stopped and turned toward Tommy and Eevie.

"Look, guys, I know I wouldn't have been your first choice to help you, but..."

Tommy cut Drew off. "Drew," he said smiling, "you would be our *only* choice."

Inside, Eevie's heart bounced. Who knew that Tommy could actually say something endearing?

Drew paused and took in what Tommy had said. He didn't have a lot of friends, and like it or not, that was one of the kindest things anyone had ever said to him. "Thanks, Tommy. Thanks, Eevie. See you guys tomorrow."

"Good night, Drew," said Tommy and Eevie in unison, and then they turned and headed toward Eevie's house.

7

PAM LEADS THEM IN THE RIGHT DIRECTION

Eevie lay in her bed reading *Percy Jackson, The Lightning Thief*. Well, that's what she wanted everyone to think she was reading. Eevie actually had hidden the spell book under the *Lightning Thief* cover.

She paused and flipped through the pages, stopping about halfway through the book. Using her phone, she took pictures of several pages of spells, and then she took photos of some of the pages that pictured a variety of plants. She uploaded them to her Google Drive, and then sent the link to Drew.

We'll figure everything out, Grandpa. Eevie's smile froze on her face. She slowly raised her eyes from her book.

Someone was staring at her through the window.

Eevie's breath caught in her throat as the shadowy figure's breath misted over the glass. Then, a bony finger traced a strange symbol into the condensation.

"Wand!" screamed Eevie. The wand instantly appeared in her hand.

"*Lucis Orbem,*" she cried out, thrusting the wand toward the window. Eevie could see the surprised look on the creature's face as the ball of light hurled toward the window, illuminating his black soulless eyes. An evil, disgusting grin filled his face, and just like that, he vanished into the night.

Eevie barely had enough time to whisper "I don't need you" before her father exploded into her room.

"Eevie," he yelled, "what's wrong?" He stared at Eevie. All of the color had drained from her face and lips.

Eevie stood trembling, staring at the window. The light from the moon shone through the hand-drawn symbol, recreating it on her desk.

"Someone was staring in my window!" she exclaimed, her voice shaking uncontrollably.

Eevie's father raced down the hallway, grabbing a flashlight and jamming bare feet into snow boots as he rushed through the front door. He slid precariously across the porch and jumped down onto the snow. His head wheeled from side to side, and he could see footsteps leading to and away from Eevie's window. *Someone had definitely been looking into Eevie's room.*

Eevie's father followed the footprints from her window to the street. A chaotic agglomeration of footprints and tire prints were mixed together; no way could he determine which way the person went.

Eevie's father gripped the Maglite tightly and returned back to the house. He cautiously circled the perimeter, searching every bush and every shadow.

Eevie's mom stood with her in the doorway, her arms wrapped protectively around her daughter's shoulders. Eevie's father reappeared, his face filled with worry.

"Eevie," he said, stepping into the house, "there are boot tracks leading from your window to the street. Are you sure you didn't get a good look at him?"

"No, he ran when I screamed," she lied.

Her heart sank; she hated having to lie to her parents. Inside she knew if her parents found out who it really was, they would never let her out of the house again—especially if they realized it was the same person who had attacked Tommy.

"They never caught the person that broke into Tommy's house," said her father, as if reading her mind. Eevie looked at her father, whose eyes burned into hers. She knew he was trying to figure out what to do.

"Maybe it was one of the neighborhood kids trying to scare me," offered Eevie. "I mean, he did run away as soon as I screamed."

"Shouldn't we call the police, Michael," asked Eevie's mom, "and at least alert them? If there is a crazy person out there, we at least owe it to our neighbors to make the police aware."

Eevie's dad nodded in agreement. "I'll go call them now..."

Eevie's heart dropped. Her parents were already reluctant about letting her go out at night...now it would be nearly impossible.

It was a full hour before Eevie's parents finally let her be by herself. She had given a carefully worded report to the police, and they had assured her parents that they would be monitoring the neighborhood for the rest of the night.

True to their word, just as Eevie sat down at her desk, a police cruiser crept by slowly. It paused in front of her house and she watched as the spotlight moved across her yard and then down and across her house. The spotlight shone on her window—revealing once again the smudged symbol the prowler had drawn.

She hadn't told the police or her parents about the symbol. It had disappeared like the ranger as the window chilled again.

Eevie didn't need to see the drawing again—it was seared into her brain. She pulled out a piece of paper and drew a circle, left open at the bottom with two *L*s facing opposite directions, composing what looked like a head, neck, and shoulders.

Now, let's see what you mean. She grabbed her phone and took a picture of her drawing and uploaded it to Google Images. Her heart pounded in her chest, making it hard for her to breathe. He had drawn the alchemy sign for death.

Eevie sat and stared at her screen until her eyes defocused into a fuzzy, pixelated blur. Her breathing slowed, and a calm resolve filled her. She clenched her jaw and smiled. She and Tommy had destroyed a spider the size of a small tank and taken down a demonic creature that would have made Voldemort soil his shorts.... *Ranger, I don't think you know who you are dealing with...*

She'd fill Tommy and Drew in on the events in the morning.

******

Tommy climbed the stairs to his room. He had just told his parents good night and opened the door when he was accosted by the smell of burning fabric. "My favorite socks!" screeched Tommy as he rushed over to his radiator.

"Oh no," he moaned. It wasn't his socks; it was Eevie's cloth. It looked like a toasted tortilla. *Eevie is going to kill me.* Tommy gently lifted the cloth, which felt brittle and delicate.

He unfolded it gingerly. He knew how much these mementos from her grandfather meant to her. *Oh man, this is*— Tommy stopped. "These aren't burn marks," he uttered, "they're numbers, and letters...." He un-folded the cloth the rest of the way. *It's some kind of map.* "Wait!" said Tommy urgently. Right before his eyes, the numbers and images began fading away. Tommy sprinted over to his workspace, brushing aside his notebook. Then as quickly as possible he carefully spread out the linen cloth on his desk. He grabbed his phone and took several pictures.

As quickly as the markings appeared, they disap-peared. He turned and looked at the radiator. "I bet the heat...the heat makes the hidden text appear," said Tommy, thinking out loud. He carefully placed the cloth on the radiator, and in a matter of moments the coffee brown numbers slowly appeared.

Tommy uploaded the pictures from his phone and opened them on his laptop. Right under the word "Pam," he saw a series of alphanumeric characters— "42.3417N70.8960W"— and below that, a series of faint lines and shapes.

Tommy opened Google and typed "42.3417N70.8960W." A single image appeared. "Dude," whispered Tommy. A map of Black Hallow Park with a tiny red pointer in the center appeared on his screen.

At the bottom of the Google map, a small icon labeled "Satellite" caught his attention. Tommy clicked the but-ton and suddenly he was staring at the rooftop of the ranger's house. He clicked the "+" button and zoomed in. He could see the ranger's car and his ATV. *Geez, if this thing zooms in any closer, I'll be able to see what he's eating for breakfast.*

Tommy's heart pounded with excitement. He flicked back to the photo he had taken. In the center of the linen cloth he çould just make out what looked like a circle and some writing, but it was too faded. He placed the cloth over the radiator once again. It darkened a little, but for some reason it still wasn't dark enough to make out. He quickly snapped a few more pictures and uploaded them to his laptop.

He tried zooming in on the image, but that only fuzzed and pixelated it more. He paused for a moment. *WWDD.* Feeling slightly nauseated at the thought of thinking like Drew, he decided that he must make sacrifices for the team, so he let his mind journey to a place it had never been before to *What Would Drew Do?* Then it hit him. *Filters...of course, filters.* They worked on his selfies. Not that Tommy relied on filters to look amazing; he *only* used filters to lower the intensity of his smile, which others had found a little too bright—or overwhelming.

My pictures should come with a warning! Never stare directly at Tommy's teeth, even with sunglasses—blindness, even death, may occur. Thank you. Ah, it's so wonderful being modest...modest and smart.

Tommy opened the photo on his phone and began applying filters when finally a sepia filter revealed the contents. He saved the changes and uploaded the image to his laptop.

"Awesome," he whispered. On the screen were three circles. At the top of the circles Tommy could barely make out the word: "Porta."

"Porta?" said Tommy, scrunching his forehead. He opened Google Translate and typed "porta." He smiled. *It means entrance or doorway!* The same series of numbers and letters 42.3417N70.8960W" appeared again, just below the three circles. There were markings inside the circle, but no matter what he tried, his ninja filter techniques were not powerful enough to reveal the hidden content.

OK, we'll worry about that part later. Right now, he needed to let the others know what he figured out. *Great news, guys, I found a secret entrance. Tiny conflict: it's in the ranger's house.*

He opened Skype and sent a group message to Drew and Eevie. "Genius alert...through the rigors of scientific process, I have discovered where our quest begins. I'll include you in the acknowledgments of my paper when published. Genius out."

As he waited for a response, he changed his Skype profile picture to Albert Einstein and in the comments he wrote: "Harvard Graduate."

Tommy leaned back in his chair, staring at his screen, and smiled. So far Tommy and his friends had been the ones being stalked and hunted like prey. It was time to turn the tables. Was it *table* or *tables*? He wasn't sure, but he knew something would be turning, and if that was a single table or many tables, that would be just fine with him.

******

Tommy's lips were vibrating. During the night, his phone had slowly inched its way down his pillow and now it lay nestled between his lips. "Argh," he said, jerking his head back, "not on a first date!"

Tommy picked up his drool-encrusted phone. *Gross.* His sleepy eyes could barely make out Eevie's smiling face on his phone screen.

"Hey, Eevie," said Tommy between yawns.

"Hey, I didn't get your Skype until this morning. You said you discovered where our quest begins?" asked Eevie excitedly. "What did you find?"

Tommy propped himself up on his elbows and shook his head to clear the cobwebs. "You know the cloth that has the initials Pam on it?"

"Ye—"

"The question is rhetorical, Eevie. I'm moving on—"

"OK," said Eevie slowly, but Tommy was already talking.

"So after you and Drew left, I was going up to my room and I smelled fabric burning. I thought it was my favorite pair of socks—you know, the ones that are black—"

"With gold lightning bolts," she said, finishing his sentence.

"Exactly, and I panicked. Not only do they make me run faster, but they're irreplaceable. They don't make them anymore."

"I wonder why...," said Eevie under her breath.

"But thank goodness it was the linen cloth," he said, "not my socks."

"What?!"

"Well, not really burning—it just smelled that way. Personally I think it was my socks, but it just so happened that the cloth had splotches of brown appearing."

"Tommy! Did you burn my grandfather's cloth?" asked Eevie with an edge to her voice.

"No! Are you kidding? There's really no need to escalate things. Geez! I clearly said splotches of brown, and just an FYI, you put the cloth on the radiator. I merely rescued it from a tragic demise. I accept paper donations in the shape of money for services rendered beyond the call of duty."

"Tommy...did you actually find anything of value...besides splotches?"

"Of course. It's what I was trying to tell you. The brown marks. When I zoomed in on them, they turned out to be a random string of letters and numbers."

"Oh, wow, another code?" asked Eevie curiously.

"I thought so, but for some reason—perhaps my inner genius bubbling to the surface played a part..." Tommy heard a muffled cough on the other end of the phone. "...I decided to Google the string of letters and numbers."

"OK, and..."

"It was map coordinates to Black Hallow Park, and when I zoomed in, the red pointer arrow was right above the ranger's house."

"How can a group of numbers make a map appear? It's not like they had computers back then? Was there anything else?"

"Yes, I won't bore you with my scientific methodology—mainly because you wouldn't understand the intricacies and nuances of my genius." Tommy paused. On the other end of the line: silence.

"OK, I'll continue," said Tommy, somewhat offended. "I used filters to darken the image on the cloth. There were three circles inside each other, and above the circles was the word 'porta'."

"A portal? You think this is the entrance to the other world?"

"I do. Well, now I do. At first I thought porta meant porta-potty, and I thought yes, that could be incredibly important. But then I of course Googled 'porta' and found that it actually meant doorway or entrance, not a temporary toilet."

"OK...," said Eevie. *Things are about to get really interesting,* she thought.

"So, my best guess is we'll find the porta somewhere inside the ranger's house."

"Tommy," said Eevie, suddenly very serious, "the ranger came to my house last night."

"What?! Are you sure?" Tommy bolted out of bed, wide awake now.

"Yes, very sure. I was reading the spell book, and for some reason I looked up and he was staring at me."

"At your window? Was he trying to get in?" Tommy's head swiveled to his window. A freezing cold finger of fear traced the length of his spine.

"He drew the alchemy symbol for death on my window."

Tommy took in a deep breath. No one was going to threaten his best friend. "Eevie, we can't just sit here and wait for something bad to happen. Somehow we need to find a way to—"

"Turn the tables?" she interjected.

"Exactly—you read my mind." Tommy made a mental note: *It was "tables"... plural.*

"That's frightening...," she said.

"Not as frightening as your face..."

"Tommy!" shouted Eevie. "I will shave your eyebrows while you sleep!"

Tommy involuntary arched his eyebrows, picturing himself eyebrowless.

"Tommy, I'm going to call Drew," said Eevie, trying to regain control of the conversation. "Can you meet at the library at eleven? That way my parents won't think I'm rushing off and become suspicious."

"Speaking of Drew, there are some questions that have been bouncing around this enormous brain of mine."

"Head," replied Eevie, unable to stop herself.

"Oh my God, I'm trying to be serious."

"Sorry," laughed Eevie. "Go ahead."

"OK. First of all, we would have never investigated the tree unless Drew had given his report about the demonic tree. We would have never found the underground labyrinth, and we would have never been nearly killed by the death zombie dude and his possessed demon monkey."

"Yeah," said Eevie, prompting him to continue.

"Then, all of the sudden, you start finding all of this stuff from your grandfather. I don't know, Eevie...it just seems a little strange to me."

"Tommy, Drew never even knew my grandfather, and a lot of people went missing at that park. It was only a matter of time before it happened again. Ironically, one of those people just happened to be in our class."

"Something just doesn't seem to fit."

"We'll figure it out, Tommy, but right now—"

"I know...right now we have a crazed ranger to deal with. Were you able to decipher any more of the book?" asked Tommy, changing the topic.

"I've deciphered two pages. Hopefully Drew has been working on what I sent him last night. I'm going to go ahead and call him, so he's not rushing. I don't want to attract any unwanted attention from the parental units."

"OK, I'll be there—I want to play with Google Maps a bit more. I have a couple ideas. Bye, Eeves."

"Bye."

8

OPERATION RANGER'S HOUSE

SURVEILLANCE

Eevie was the first to arrive at the Donovan Haw-thorne Library. A bespectacled, middle-aged woman sat impossibly upright at the head of a huge horseshoe-shaped circulation desk. *She looks like the captain of a ship,* thought Eevie.

Eevie's smile was met with watchful eyes that peered over black cat-eye glasses. She felt the librarian's gaze follow her like a cloud as she walked to the study area at the back of the library.

Eevie spotted a long, wooden table nestled in the cor-ner, with two huge, fungus green-colored overstuffed armchairs.

She had just placed her backpack on the table and was about to text Tommy and Drew when they walked in together.

"This room smells like wet newspaper," said Tommy.

Several patrons looked up from their books and stared at Tommy. Their eyes filled with disdain for his abrupt interruption of their solitude.

"Sorry," whispered Drew, who pointed at Tommy. "He's *new* to knowledge."

"Wow, guys," said Eevie, shaking her head, "way to not bring attention to us."

"Sorry," Tommy quietly said, placing his backpack beside Eevie's.

"OK," said Drew, leaning in and speaking in a hushed tone, "catch me up on what's going on."

Tommy opened his laptop and spent the next several minutes showing Drew and Eevie what he had discovered.

"Those numbers stand for latitude and longitude," said Drew as Tommy showed him the satellite photos of the ranger's house.

"Oh, cool," said Eevie, nodding, "and those circles, we think, are the secret entranceway to...well...somewhere. We're not sure where yet."

Drew reached in his backpack and pulled out a stack of papers.

"Eevie," said Drew quietly, "the pictures that you sent to me are plants that are used for different—*potions*. Each one does something different."

"Like this one, Aqua Cicuta," said Drew as he pulled a page from the stack. At the top of the page Drew had sketched the plant and written the description of the potion below it.

"For this one, you can grind the roots and the stem into a liquid paste. It can then be dissolved into tea or even baked into bread. There is no antidote, and if it doesn't kill you, you are likely to suffer from amnesia the rest of your life."

"Eeesh," said Tommy, "so you wouldn't even remember what gave you amnesia."

Drew looked at Eevie as if to say, *Please tell me he is kidding.*

"Anyways," continued Drew as he slid the stack of papers over to Eevie, "I translated all of the pages with the plants for you."

"Thank you so much, Drew," said Eevie, patting him on the shoulder. "That's a huge help!"

"Sorry," said Tommy, snapping his fingers in Drew's face, "back to reality. Eevie, I would be careful accepting any food or drinks from Drew. There was probably a love potion he conveniently left out of the stack."

"No," said Drew, "but there is one that will paralyze you temporarily while you can still feel everything. You just need to let the leaves dry and then grind them into a fine powder." He held out his hand, his palm facing the ceiling. "Then, you just blow like this."

He pretended to blow powder into Tommy's face.

Several people looked up, staring at the boys. Tommy nodded, acknowledging their attention, and pointed toward Drew. "He's blowing me kisses again. What can I say? He's incorrigible and I'm irresistible."

Drew's face reddened. "I was not blowing you kisses. I was paralyzing you, and you're not my type."

"Tommy, seriously?" said Eevie, disapprovingly. "These potions could be incredibly important to us. It probably took Drew hours to figure all of this out. You should be thanking him, not ridiculing him."

"It's cool," said Drew, raising his hands. "I worked through the night on them. I thought with everything going on, sooner would be better than later. Tommy's just being Tommy."

"And by being Tommy, you mean awesome."

Tommy was about to continue when Eevie's eyes gave him the zip-it-or-face-my-wrath stare.

Tommy just now noticed the dark purple shadows under Drew's eyes and his hunched demeanor. *Dang, I'm a jerk. I guess he did work through the night.*

"Thank you, Drew," said Tommy. "I can tell you put in a crazy amount of work on these, and they look awesome. Sorry for being such a jerk."

Drew nodded and smiled a tired smile. "Thanks, Tommy."

"All right," said Eevie, turning her legal pad lengthwise. "One, we need to figure out how to get to, and then into, the ranger's house without being seen. Two, we need to find the secret doorway, and figure out what to do once we find it. We also need to figure out what we need to bring. Last time we were completely unprepared."

"Last time we didn't realize we were gonna be ripped from the face of the earth," said Tommy as he arched his eyebrows.

"We need to find out if the ranger has a schedule. He has to. He's the one who checks to make sure everyone leaves at closing time. He's the one who locks the gate. That's our window of opportunity. He's probably out of his house for twenty minutes at least," said Drew.

"OK, perfect, so he's away from the house. But how do we get in? I'm pretty sure he's not gonna just leave the door open," said Tommy matter-of-factly.

Tommy opened the Google satellite picture again and switched to street view. The ranger's house appeared at ground level. "Well, he has two windows on the front of the house, so I'm guessing there are a couple on the back," Tommy said. "Our best chance is to go through one of the back windows."

"Our window of opportunity," smiled Eevie.

"Drew could hide and keep us updated on the ranger via our phones. If we need to get out, Drew could let us know," said Tommy.

"So, we simply have to find the secret passage, and then what?" Eevie asked while stretching.

"Well…," said Tommy, pausing, "we see where it goes."

"Tommy, you do realize if we get trapped, or locked in, and have to wait until the next day when the ranger leaves, our lives are over."

Tommy nodded. "We just need to make sure that that doesn't happen," he answered reassuringly. "OK, we've got a plan for getting in, and searching for the entrance. We just need to figure out what to bring, and it looks like we need to do a little spying on the ranger to find out his routine," continued Tommy.

"Leave that to me," smiled Drew. "If anyone catches you near that park again, your parents will never let you leave your house."

Tommy looked at Drew, his eyes filled with respect. "All right, Drew, our lives and freedom depend on your expert surveillance! Make us proud!"

"Tommy," said Eevie, "if you can figure out what you think we'll need to bring, I'll focus on deciphering and learning as many of those spells as I can. I caught the ranger off guard once. This time I fear he'll be ready."

9

Don't Forget to Delete Your Browser History

Four days had passed since the meeting at the Donovan Hawthorne Library. The three agreed to have very little contact so they didn't draw any unnecessary attention to themselves. More importantly, they wanted to make sure that Drew had sufficient time to establish the ranger's routine. Each night they would meet on Skype video to fill each other in on their accomplishments.

Drew looked like he was about to explode. So Eevie, who looked unusually exhausted, asked him to go first.

"Alright," said Drew excitedly, "the ranger definitely has a pattern. About twenty-five minutes before the park closes, he jumps onto his ATV and disappears down the trails for about twenty minutes. He then sits by the front gate and waits for everyone to leave. As soon as everyone is out of the park, he wraps the chain around the gate, locks it, parks his ATV, and goes back inside."

"So just to be safe, the most we have is probably twenty-five minutes, with a tiny five-minute safety buffer. Problem is, getting out of the park," said Eevie.

"Not a problem," said Drew, smiling. "I'll be monitoring you guys from outside, and I'll have this in my backpack." Drew held up a huge knotted rope for Eevie and Tommy to see. "I'll throw this over the wall so you guys can climb out."

"Drew, you win the genius T-shirt. Great job!" beamed Eevie. Tommy was nodding his head as well. *They had twenty-five minutes—that should be plenty of time.*

"What did you find out, Tommy?" asked Drew.

"So, first let me say, I had to delete my Google search history because my parents would have launched my computer out the window. I Googled how to pick locks, how to break into a window, and extreme survival gear."

"Just what parents want to find on their teenage son's computer," said Eevie.

"The window is definitely gonna be our best and safest option," said Tommy, continuing. "I did learn a cool trick on the special ops website. It said to not only have a backpack with you, but also to duct tape things to your first layer of clothing, like another flashlight, lighter, knife, etc. Lastly, I also bought two black, military-grade, slimline, waterproof backpacks from Amazon. I'm going to hope my genius IQ gets me a scholarship because I just spent all of my money on these bad boys." Tommy held them up to his camera.

"Woah!" exclaimed Drew. "Nice!"

"All right, Eeves, dazzle us with what you found out," said Tommy anxiously.

"So," Eevie slowly began, "I've deciphered just about every spell in the book." She paused, her face filling with disappointment. "But I must be doing something wrong. The first two spells work perfectly, but the others...I can't seem to get them to work. I think my wand is even frustrated with me."

"Eevie," smiled Tommy reassuringly, "you're the smartest girl I know, and I know like fifteen—maybe more. It's probably just something simple. You'll figure it out! Plus, you finished figuring out the rest of the book—you've got to be exhausted."

Eevie nodded. She had barely slept. "I know," she said, but she couldn't help feeling frustrated and a little afraid that...maybe she wouldn't be able to get the spells to work.

"You'll get it, Eevie. You just need some rest," said Drew reassuringly.

Eevie nodded in thanks.

"OK," said Drew, looking at his friends to make sure he had their attention. "On the park's website, it says Saturday is their busiest day. If we're lucky, that may even buy you guys a couple extra minutes of time."

Tommy nodded in agreement. Saturday was two days away. "OK," said Tommy, his eyes staring into his best friend's eyes. He could see the fear and the exhaustion. "Everyone, get as much rest as you can tonight and tomorrow. Saturday will be here before you know it. Good night, guys."

"Good night," said Drew and Eevie in unison.

Tommy texted Eevie an emoji with little hearts circling around it, and typed: *Please get some rest—we'll figure this out together, we always do.* He closed the lid of his laptop and climbed into bed. *Here we go again...here we go.*

10

THE RANGER MUST BE A MINIMALIST

If skies had personalities, this one was definitely sulking. Gray clouds like puffed-up cheeks threatened to spew icy rain onto the trio as they biked to the delicious but not so nutritious Donut Shack.

Eevie and Tommy hid their bikes behind Donut Shack's giant blue dumpster, which was hidden from view by a tall, wooden fence. And, thanks to Drew's reconnaissance, they knew that the trash company would not be by to empty it until Tuesday.

The small café was buzzing with activity, as festive holiday music descended upon them from tiny silver circular speakers. The aroma of coffee and fresh baked goods seemed at odds with their current state of mind.

"Listen," said Tommy as he attempted to casually slide across a sticky, burgundy, half-moon-shaped vinyl cushion. "I've come up with a name for us. We can be known as TED." Tommy looked at his friends expectantly.

Eevie and Drew returned his stare with expressions that said, *What did I do wrong in my life to deserve this?*

"Get it? Tommy, Eevie, and Drew. The first letter of each of our names spells T-E-D." His voice trailed off.

"TED," he said softly, looking from Eevie to Drew. "Awe, come on, guys, our names," he said, crestfallen.

"It's a great idea, Tommy," said Eevie, gently smiling at her friend. "But I'm not really in the mood to laugh or make jokes. We *really* need to focus. I mean—*laser* focus. We can't mess up this time. We can't afford to get caught. We'll be trespassing, breaking the law, going into the house of a crazed man who tried to kill you. And if all of that wasn't bad enough, if something happens..." Eevie's voice cracked, "...our parents will never trust us again."

Tommy slowly put his hands around his cup of coffee, interlacing his fingers. It was a bit too hot to hold, but for some reason it calmed him. Drew sat silently, thinking, taking everything in.

"All right," said Tommy, "I was just trying to lighten the mood a little."

Drew smiled. "You're a good friend, Tommy." He paused. "Guys, it's 3:40," he said, looking down at his Apple watch. "The park closes at 4:30. We need to get ready because the ranger will be leaving his house in about twenty minutes."

Tommy put a $10 bill under his coffee cup. As they stood to leave, Frank Sinatra's "I'll Be Home for Christmas" drifted through the café. Eevie closed her eyes as raw emotion filled her heart.

******

Tommy and Eevie pulled their hoodies over their heads. They stood diagonal to the park's main entrance, waiting for an opportunity to sneak across the street and hide without being seen. Drew had already slipped across the street and was lying flat on the icy ground, hidden from view.

"Go!" whispered Drew urgently.

Tommy and Eevie raced across the street, then dove behind a large clump of bushes just as a group of people walked out the gate.

"That was a little too close," said Tommy, quietly watching the group turn and walk toward the bus station.

Eevie jumped as her phone gently vibrated against her leg. She could hear Drew's voice in her earbud. Tommy's phone vibrated next as Drew conferenced him in.

"Can everyone hear each other?" asked Drew.

"I can hear you, Drew," said Eevie quietly.

"It's as if you were right here," said Tommy.

Eevie smacked Tommy on the back of the head. "Be serious!"

"Fine," said Tommy, looking at Eevie. "That's an affirmative."

"You guys stay down. I have a clear view of the ranger's house," said Drew. "Remember, as soon as you go through the gate run to the left. He has a huge pile of logs stacked about fifty feet from his house. I'll let you know as soon as he leaves. Remember, leave your phone on!"

"OK," said Eevie, "sounds good."

Tommy gave a thumbs-up.

"He can't see you, Tommy," moaned Eevie. "Oh, God, we're doomed."

Drew looked at his watch: 3:55 p.m. A flow of cars and pedestrians were steadily streaming out of the park. Then he saw him. The ranger was limping toward his ATV. Drew's heart began pounding in his chest like an angry neighbor.

"Guys," Drew said, his voice wavering with nervous energy, "he's leaving now."

"OK," Eevie acknowledged. "Let us know when it's clear."

"Go…NOW!" Drew commanded.

Eevie and Tommy raced down the icy sidewalk, slipping and sliding through the gate. They were completely relying on Drew to get them to the woodpile unseen.

"Go, go, go!" exclaimed Drew. "Down, down!"

Eevie and Tommy dropped flat to the ground as if they were about to be raked by enemy fire. However, this full-frontal assault came in the form of a silver Honda Accord. Tommy watched as the car slowly took the curve and then stopped alongside where they lay in the snow, just inside the front gate.

"No way they're not going to see us," whispered Eevie.

They watched in horror as a man and woman wearing matching white puffy winter coats and what appeared to be brown fluffy winter hats adorned with reindeer antlers quickly clambered out of their car.

"Oh, great," whispered Tommy. "He's pulling out his phone—we're so dead."

"Blend with the terrain," said Eevie through gritted teeth. "Blend into your environment."

"How?" whispered Tommy without moving his lips. "We're literally laying on a huge white blanket of snow.

Eevie didn't answer as she lay motionless. Tommy surreptitiously placed a tiny dead tree branch across his face. The only thing that moved was Tommy's eyes— and they didn't like what they saw.

The man and woman turned and looked at the ranger's house. Eevie and Tommy lay out in the open, holding their breath, willing themselves to be invisible.

The man held up his phone in the universal selfie position as his companion lay her head on his shoulder. Flash! The couple jolted their heads back simultaneously, and then broke into spontaneous laughter. The man hunched over and appeared to be fiddling with his phone. The woman leaned in and gave him a peck on his cheek. Tommy and Eevie let out a sigh of relief when they heard the soft *ding-ding* chime of the doors opening.

"Rookies. They're probably too blinded by the flash to see anything..." Eevie was proven correct when the man nearly drove into the gate as they left.

"Thank goodness for narcissism," whispered Tommy.

Eevie turned and looked at Tommy, bewildered.

"What? I have a massive vocabulary." She didn't believe him. "Fine," said Tommy, "it was on my Word of the Day calendar."

"Sorry to interrupt, but..."

Before Drew could finish his sentence, Tommy and Eevie were already up, sprinting to their next hiding place. They kneeled, hidden behind a massive pile of snow-covered logs. They slowly raised their heads, taking in their surroundings. In the distance they could see cars and people exiting the park. No one was looking their way.

"All right," said Tommy, touching Eevie's shoulder. "Let's go!"

Eevie and Tommy dashed through the woods until they were safely behind the ranger's house. Tommy gently placed his ear against the cold wooden panels and listened intently. There was no sound coming from inside.

"It sounds empty," he said. "I don't hear anything."

"OK, guys, you have twenty-five minutes tops," said Drew excitedly.

Tommy snuck quietly to the front of the house and climbed the wooden railing onto the front porch. Kneeling low, he tried twisting the front doorknob and pushing. The door didn't budge. He leaned over the railing and gave Eevie the thumbs-down. "Locked," said Tommy disappointedly.

"OK," whispered Drew, "plan B."

Eevie looked up at the windows. There were two of them, and they were both about five feet off the ground.

"They didn't look this high in the picture...," said Tommy.

"It's fine. Let's just see if they're unlocked."

Tommy leaned against the house and interlocked his fingers, creating a foothold for Eevie. She placed her right foot on Tommy's makeshift step and, using her left foot, propelled herself up. The window was divided into two sections of four glass panes. She dug her fingers on the bottom edge of the frame and pulled upward. The window creaked and groaned, but it wouldn't budge.

She looked down at Tommy, frustrated. "I think it's locked."

He nodded. "Let's try the other one," he said.

They hurried over to the next window, repeating the same pattern. This time Eevie banged her fist against the window and tried prying it and then hitting the frame with her palms, but no matter how hard she pulled and pushed, the window stood its ground. "It's no use," she said angrily. "They're locked."

"Eevie, I have an idea. Give me just a second."

Tommy ran into the woods, then returned carrying a log and large rock.

"Tommy, what are you doing?"

"Look, the ranger broke into my house and tried to kill me. He threatened to kill you." Anger flashed in Tommy's eyes. "A *window* is not going to stop us."

Tommy reached into his backpack and pulled out a roll of black duct tape. He tore off two ten-inch strips of tape with his teeth and stuck them to the front of his hoodie, then handed Eevie the roll of tape.

Eevie watched silently as Tommy placed the log under the window and then climbed on top. He steadied himself and then, one at a time, he pulled the strip of tape from his hoodie and made an *X* across the glass pane. Eevie grabbed him by the waist to help support him.

"Everything OK?" asked Drew into their earbuds.

"We're OK," said Eevie, concentrating. "We'll let you know as soon as we are inside."

Tommy reached into his front pocket and pulled out the rock he'd found. He smacked it against the window in the center of the taped "X." There was a sharp crack as the glass shattered.

The duct tape did its job, the sound was minimal, and glass shards didn't rain down on top of them. Tommy carefully reached through the broken pane and turned the lock. He put the rock back into his pocket and then pushed on the window. The window shuddered and moved just a hair. From the amount of cobwebs, Tommy observed that, *he probably hadn't opened these things in years*.

"Twenty minutes." Drew's voice echoed in their ears.

"Tommy, we're running out of time," said Eevie, her voice full of worry.

Tommy smashed the heels of his palms upward into the wooden frame. The window moved up a few inches. "Yes!" he exclaimed.

He drove his hand upward again, and finally the window acquiesced. He gripped the bottom frame and visualized himself curling a thousand pounds. The window shot up, slamming the top of the frame.

"I got it," said Tommy excitedly. "It's open!"

"I heard," said Drew. "I think they heard that two states away."

Tommy dropped to the ground. He was about to ask Eevie if she was ready, but she was already on the log pulling herself up. Eevie's feet kicked out, as she used the toes of her shoes on the wall to propel herself upward.

Tommy cupped his hands under her kicking feet and lifted, perhaps a little too hard, causing Eevie to torpedo through the window. He cringed as he heard a loud *oomph* and several additional crashes that sounded like furniture falling and glass breaking.

"Eevie...," cried Tommy through clenched teeth as he clambered up the log. "Eevie, are you OK?"

Tommy pulled himself up through the broken window. On the floor lay Eevie, staring up at the ceiling. A small, broken table lay on top of her, and a shattered picture frame lay on the floor just past her head.

"Eevie?"

"I'm OK," she half-groaned, half-whispered.

"Thank God," said Tommy, his voice filled with relief.

"Tommy, remember when you said tables would be turning?"

"Yeah," said Tommy.

Eevie pushed the table off her chest. "I didn't realize you meant that literally."

Tommy smiled. This is why he loved Eevie.

Eevie helped Tommy through the window into what appeared to be the ranger's office.

"What's happening?" asked Drew, still plenty worried.

"I accidentally launched Eevie, but she's fine."

"I'm fine, Drew," said Eevie. "We're both inside."

A single bare bulb illuminated what appeared to be a very sparsely furnished office. The creepiness factor was indeed a trend the ranger decided to embrace in all parts of his life. Starting with his furniture. Against the back wall, a battered desk supported an old computer system with a very loose fan that hummed continuously like a small prop plane. In an adjacent corner stood a tall, narrow bookshelf.

"Sheesh, this guy clearly isn't a fan of home decorating shows. Is that a stuffed badger in his window?" asked Tommy. "That's just creepy."

"Drew, keep us updated," said Eevie. "We're gonna look for the secret passage."

"OK, good luck. You have about fifteen minutes left."

"There are a few more rooms, Drew. We're gonna split up and see what we can find," said Tommy.

"OK," said Drew. "No sign of him yet, and people are still leaving."

"Tommy, you take the back of the house," said Eevie while walking toward the kitchen. "I'll take the front."

Tommy pulled out his flashlight. He didn't want to turn on any lights in the house and alert the ranger to their presence. He walked through a small hallway. "Found his bedroom," said Tommy. He turned slowly in a circle. *Obviously this guy is a minimalist*, he thought. There was a very simple bed that oddly looked like it hadn't been slept in...ever...and a small closet. Tommy slowly opened the door to the closet. Inside were two green jackets adorned with Black Hallow Park emblems and a badge, two dark green shirts, and two pairs of khaki pants. A pair of boots lay on the floor at the foot of his bed.

Tommy quickly began checking for a hidden doorway. He slid the clothes aside and pushed and knocked on the walls. He pushed at the top of boards and at the bottom. Nothing. Next he pulled the ranger's bed from the wall and rapped on the floorboards with his knuckles—nothing sounded unusual, nothing moved.

"Nothing back here," said Tommy. "How about you, Eevie?"

"I checked the kitchen and the bathroom."

"Did you push on the walls—and all the boards?" he asked.

"I pushed and pulled on everything. I even flushed his toilet..."

"That's going beyond the call of duty," snickered Tommy. "Get it...duty?"

"Tommy!"

"I'm sorry, I'm sorry!" he sputtered. "I talk when I'm nervous."

"Guys, he's pulling up to the gate!" Drew warned. "I see a few more people leaving, but you don't have long!"

Eevie and Tommy crawled over to the window in front of the desk. They could see the ranger sitting on his ATV as the last groups of stragglers left the park. Eevie looked at Tommy. "We've got to hurry!"

Immediately they dropped to the floor, hitting each board with balled-up fists. Eevie eyed the ranger's desk. "Tommy why would he have a rug under his desk?"

"To protect the floor from his chair. My dad has one under his chair."

"Yeah, but not the whole desk."

They raced over to the desk. Eevie slid the chair aside and lifted a corner of the rug.

"Darn it," Eevie said, frowning. "Looks like the rest of the floor."

Undeterred, Tommy slid the desk backwards and yanked the rug, sending it sliding across the floor. Eevie crawled forward and hit the flooring with her hand. She paused, then hit the floor once more.

Tommy pulled out his pocketknife and drove the blade between the floorboards. *Did they just move?* He stabbed his knife deep into the wooden plank and pulled. The skewered board came up easily. In the dim lighting they could just make out something beneath.

"Drew, we found something! Where's the ranger?" asked Eevie.

"He's still at the gate. The last couple is about to leave!"

Now that the plank was missing, it was easy to re-move the rest of the boards. In a matter of seconds, a huge recessed circle was revealed. Tommy shone his flashlight on the circle to get a better look. It was made up of three concentric rings, and each ring was engraved with a series of cryptic symbols.

"It looks like a giant astrolabe!" said Eevie excitedly. "Except this one has different images."

"Not all of them are different," said Tommy. "Look at the second row. Those are the symbols for the constellations."

Eevie reached out. "The circles turn," she said. "I bet we have to align it correctly, like a giant combination lock."

"Hurry!" said Drew. "Everyone's gone!"

"Drew, there are some symbols and we have no idea what they are. Can you help?" asked Eevie frantically.

"Quick, send me a picture?" whispered Drew urgently.

Tommy pulled out his phone and took a picture of the circle and sent it to Drew.

Seconds later, Drew's phone vibrated.

"Give me just a second," said Drew, opening the image. "OK, the first circle is made up of the planets, the second circle is constellations, and the third circle has constellations as well.... There doesn't seem to be any pattern. Are there any other markings I'm not seeing?"

"No," said Eevie. "Not that we see." Drew could hear the panic building in her voice.

"Wait!" said Drew excitedly. "They are all planets, except for one, the sun. The sun is a star."

Eevie immediately turned the first circle, aligning the sun to the top. Nothing happened. Eevie touched the sun. The engraved section sank down, about a millimeter, making a soft mechanical click. The outermost wheel locked into place.

"It worked!" exclaimed Tommy excitedly.

Drew looked up from his hiding spot, about ten feet from the front gate. He could hear the metallic clanking of the chain as the ranger wrapped it around the post of the gate. He could see the smoke rising around his face with each breath.

"He's putting the chain on the gate," said Drew in hushed tones. "You've literally got about two minutes."

"What about the second wheel?" asked Eevie, her voice filled with urgency. "Anything that doesn't belong there?"

"Forget about that," said Tommy. He began moving the wheel and pressing each image.

"He's done locking the gate!" bellowed Drew. "I'm gonna distract him!"

"Distract him? What do you mean distract him?" asked Tommy, confused. "You're gonna get yourself killed."

"Just do what you gotta do," said Drew. "I'll try to buy you as much time as I can!"

Eevie ran over to the window. In the distance, she could see the ranger climbing onto his ATV. She rushed back over to Tommy, begging time to slow down.

Tommy spun the second circle, pausing only for a millisecond to press each constellation symbol. His hand froze as the serpent constellation pressed into place.

They could hear Drew's breathing; it sounded like he was running. What they didn't know was that Drew had been hurling rocks at the ranger, one of which finally hit its mark. It smacked the ranger in the back of the head just as he was turning toward his house.

They heard Drew's voice through their earbuds. "Oh, sorry. Did I do that?" More bursts of heavy breathing.

Eevie's hands were shaking. "The third circle doesn't move and there's nothing to press!"

Tommy stared at the circle, his mind racing at lightning speed. "Of course!" He jumped to his feet and tore into his backpack, pulling out the astrolabe. He placed it into the center circle; it fit perfectly.

Tommy turned the astrolabe slowly, aligning the three openings with the three star systems they had aligned earlier. "Gemini, Cancer, Canis Minor," whispered Tommy. This time there was a much louder metallic click, like the sound of a safe opening.

"You did it!" exclaimed Eevie.

Outside, the ranger climbed off his ATV and smiled at Drew. Rivulets of black blood ran down the side of his neck, staining his collar. Suddenly, inside Drew's head, an evil voice filled his mind. *I know why you're here...and now, Drew, I'm going to kill your friends and then I'm going to kill you. Don't fall asleep tonight...*

Drew clutched the bars of the gate, shaking them and screaming, "I'm not afraid of you!" He watched in horror as the ranger turned and began quickly limping toward the house.

"Hey!" screamed Drew desperately, but he watched helplessly as the ranger continued toward the house. Drew fell against the gate, gagging. He turned and retched. He could barely whisper the words as his heart beat rapidly. "He's coming...! He knows."

Drew collapsed onto the ground in front of the gate. *They are going to die—and it's all my fault.*

Eevie scrambled to the window. She could see a figure limping toward the house—it was like a scene from a horror movie. Running to the kitchen, she grabbed a chair and forcefully wedged it underneath the doorknob. She reached into her backpack and pulled out a long coil of rope. She tied a loop around the doorknob and threaded the remainder around the refrigerator, in hopes of preventing the ranger from pulling the door open. She pulled the rope taut, tied another knot, and ran back to Tommy.

Tommy had opened the secret doorway, and stale, musty air rushed out at them, burning their nostrils.

"OK, Eevie," said Tommy, turning to her. "We have two options. We go in, and we have no idea what will happen to us..." Tommy looked down into the blackness. "Or as soon as he starts coming in, we jump out the window."

"No, Tommy," said Eevie firmly. "He'll know we found the portal. We won't ever get another chance."

"OK," said Tommy, pausing and reaching out his hand, grabbing hers. "For your grandpa."

Eevie stared deep into Tommy's eyes. "For Grandpa."

The sudden sound of the doorknob turning was deafening. They didn't want to look, but their eyes betrayed them. Staring at them through the thin rectangular sliver of glass was the ranger. The door shook violently, straining against the frame, as he tried over and over to get in.

Tommy shone his flashlight into the opening, revealing a small, black, iron ladder. "Go! Eevie, go!" Tommy shouted. She slid her feet over the edge, inching closer as she kicked out, trying to find the first rung. She exhaled sharply as her feet finally made solid contact with the ladder. She paused for a second, getting her bearings, and then began quickly descending into the darkness below.

"Get the astrolabe!" yelled Eevie up to Tommy.

Tommy twisted and pulled, but the astrolabe would not come free. *I bet I'd have to close the portal to remove the astrolabe. But then Eevie would be locked down there and...*

Smash! Tommy looked up as the glass in the door shattered. He saw the ranger thrust his hand through the broken pane, pulling the chair away from beneath the door handle.

There was no way he could break the astrolabe free in time. Tommy rolled onto his stomach and slid his legs into the inky blackness. He quickly climbed down a couple rungs, reached up, and slammed the portal door closed.

"Eevie, are you OK?" His voice echoed off the walls of the tunnel. Tommy wrapped one arm around the ladder for support, then shone his flashlight below him.

"I'm good," she called back, her voice trembling.

"Just concentrate on climbing down," Tommy called back. "I'm right behind you. Drew knows we are here— we'll be OK!"

Tommy placed his flashlight between his teeth and continued descending, being careful not to step on Eevie's fingers. They continued downward in silence, the only sound being the soft metallic clangs that rose through the air with every step.

Eevie slowed her descent as she became aware of a pale yellow light.

"Tommy," she called up softly.

"I see it," he replied before she could finish. "Light!"

The ranger used a piece of broken glass to slash through the rope tied around the door handle, then burst into the house.

"Tommy, Eevie...where are you?" he demanded, his voice cutting and shrill like fingernails scraping down a chalkboard. He smiled a black, bloody smile as he limped into his office. They had found the secret passage, but they were trapped and there was no way out.

11

COILED AGAIN!

Eevie froze. Bones lay scattered across the dirt floor...human bones. Tilting her head back, she put her index finger to her lips. Tommy nodded silently. Cautiously, Eevie stepped onto the dirt floor. She watched as Tommy quickly but quietly made his way down.

"It looks like a dungeon," she whispered.

Tommy simply nodded as he scanned the room.

The walls were muddy brown. Chunks of gray and brown stone jutted outward, making the walls look like giant chocolate chip cookies. Flames flickered in black oil lanterns dancing to their own music, casting a mosaic of shadows. Their eyes followed the row of candles to the end of the narrow cavern, where the wall was solid black. The surface was much different than the rest of the cave. It shimmered as if breathing.

Tommy knelt. Shallow furrows snaked along the dirt floor into the darkness—it looked like someone had rolled a large barrel in a series of connected *S*'s down the length of the cavern. His eyes traced the curious pattern. Tommy blinked. Did he see a flicker of red light?

"Eevie," whispered Tommy, trying to calm himself, "something doesn't feel right."

"I know." Eevie's senses were on high alert. Every sound, every shadow drew her in. "Tommy, you try to find a way out. I think it's best if I stand guard."

"OK, good idea," he said. "This place creeps me out."

Eevie watched and listened intently as Tommy began slowly moving down the wall. His hands moved methodically—up and down the walls, pushing and pulling each rock, looking for a way out.

Eevie shook her head. *Had one of the lanterns gone out?* She stared intently. *Probably ran out of oil,* she thought in an attempt to reassure herself. *Wait, it's lit again...now the one in front of it is out....* Then she saw it.

Eevie's scream pierced Tommy's spine like a thousand shards of glass.

He stumbled backwards, smacking his head against a low-hanging rock. Through a flash of stars, he could just make out a huge, black silhouette of a snake filling the hallway. The shadow moved closer. Now he knew what had made those grooves on the dirt floor.

The snake's black and silver head was the size of a small car. Curved, razor-sharp fangs dripped with poison as if the snake was salivating—thinking of its next meal. The light from the lanterns made its blood-red eyes look like they were made of liquid fire. A massive forked tongue flicked out, toward Eevie, tasting the air as its eyes narrowed in on her.

"Eevie!" screamed Tommy as the snake struck out with incredible speed. Eevie dropped flat to the ground.

Pieces of rock and wall exploded into the air as the snake's fangs drove deep into the wall just above her head.

Tommy yelled, jumping up and down, waving his arms, trying to give Eevie a chance to get to her feet. Eevie scrambled, running toward Tommy, but she didn't make it. The impact from the second attack was so brutal that Eevie nearly lost consciousness. The snake used its head like a fist, pounding her into the ground.

Tommy ripped his knife from his belt and charged the snake. He stabbed furiously into its body, but its scales were impenetrable. Every strike sent a painful shock up Tommy's arm.

Switching tactics, Tommy wrapped his arms around the snake's powerful body, trying in vain to distract it and keep it from attacking Eevie again as she crawled on hands and feet to the back of the cavern.

The snake tore through Tommy's grip and struck again, its fangs driving into Eevie's back. She screamed, her arms and legs flailing as she felt hot liquid course down her back and legs.

"Tommy," she whispered as tears filled her eyes. The snake whipped her like a rag doll, and then she was still.

Tommy raced to the ladder, bounding up the steps. He grabbed an oil lantern, ripping and pulling with superhuman strength. He pried it from the wall—and then, without a second of hesitation, he jumped from the ladder onto the serpent's back.

The snake whipped its body back and forth, trying to dislodge him. Tommy gripped the lantern between his teeth, and hand over hand he hauled himself up the snake's body to his head.

"Eevie!" shouted Tommy desperately. His voice echoed back at him, as if mocking him.

Holding his body flush against the snake's head, he pulled out his knife and, using the butt, shattered the oil lamp's glass globe. Hot oil spat from the lamp onto his hand and the snake, instantly burning and blistering them.

The snake slammed its head sideways against the wall, and Tommy took the full force of the blow on his shoulder. He heard and felt a loud crunch, as pain shot through his body. Tommy's arm hung useless across his chest, as he clenched his teeth, breathing through the pain. Eevie's body hung limp, impaled by the serpent's fangs. Venom ran down her arms and dripped from her fingertips.

As the snake coiled back to lash out again, Tommy flattened his body against it. This time the snake thrust its head upward, trying to crush him against a jagged outcrop of rocks. Rolling to the side of the snake's head, he narrowly avoided being crushed into oblivion.

Tommy's jaws and lips were bloody and torn, and hot oil had splashed onto his face and neck. Squeezing and driving upward with his legs, he lunged forward and drove his knife into the snake's eye. The snake hissed and growled in pain, as Tommy tipped the oil lantern over and poured hot, fiery oil into the hollow of the snake's eye.

Writhing in pain, the snake shook its head and slammed itself from side to side. Explosions of rock fragment and dirt filled the cave. Tommy leapt from the snake's back and landed hard, with pain burning up his shoulder into his skull.

Tommy ran toward the snake, its head hung low, while Eevie dangled precariously from its fangs.

"Eevie!" Tommy yelled, hoping for any sign of life.

The snake lunged at Tommy, and he ducked as he felt a rush of air pass over him. Out of the corner of his eye he saw Eevie's eyes flash open.

Eevie twisted, still impaled by the snake's fangs. Her head lolled forward as a wave of dizziness passed over her.

"Eevie!" screamed Tommy, his face twisted, filled with raw emotion. "Hang on!"

Tommy moved himself into the snake's strike zone. "Come on!" screamed Tommy. "Come on!"

The snake lashed out, but Tommy was already jumping. He grabbed hold of Eevie and pulled down on her, sending them both crashing to the ground. Tommy clenched his teeth as he flickered back and forth between consciousness and unconsciousness.

Another shadow had joined them in the cavern. The ranger was quickly climbing down the ladder.

"Eevie, we've gotta run! The ranger's here."

Tommy pulled Eevie to her feet with his good arm, just as the ranger's boots hit the ground. Tommy kicked into a pile of dirt and rock, sending it into the ranger's face. The ranger screamed, wiping the dirt from his eyes. "It's going to be a pleasure killing you," he said, his voice icy and cold.

The snake's head swung like a broken pendulum, its head crashing into the walls of the cavern. Lanterns fell to the floor, their fiery oil spreading like lava as black clouds of smoke engulfed them.

Eevie and Tommy backed away, coughing and wiping at their eyes. But it was no use; their backs slammed against the wall. They had reached the end of the cave, and there was nothing left to do but fight.

Eevie held her battered forearm across her face trying to keep the smoke from her eyes. Through the flames, she could make out the ranger limping toward them, his mouth upturned in an evil smile—and in his hand, the largest knife she had ever seen.

"You'll never get away with this!" spat Eevie. "The police will be here any second."

The snake was so close now that its tongue flickered merely inches from their faces. The ranger stopped beside the giant serpent. "Ahriman," he whispered, as he stared at Tommy and Eevie, "kill them!"

The snake struck with lightning speed. Tommy tackled Eevie hard to the ground as the snake's fangs struck the wall. A loud crashing sound reverberated through the cave, as the back wall shattered, crumbling onto them.

Light poured into the cave. Tommy reached out and grabbed Eevie, pulling her through the opening.

"NO!" screamed the ranger.

Pure adrenaline coursed through them. They turned, expecting the ranger to be right behind them, except the wall that had shattered just a moment earlier instantly flew back together into one solid piece. They stared in utter amazement, the shimmering black stone wall had turned into a solid curtain of transparent rock. Eevie and Tommy gasped in horror as the ranger slammed his palms against the wall, which shook under his on-slaught. He pressed his face against the wall. As he did so, the human skin melted from his face like wax dripping from a candle, revealing a twisted white face. His black, soulless eyes stared at them, while his black, oily mouth—filled with spike-chiseled teeth—sneered at them.

Tommy and Eevie shivered. At least they were safe for now—or so they thought. The ranger's fingers ripped through his human facade, boring into the curtain of rock that separated them. Eevie grabbed Tommy by his injured shoulder. He howled in pain, just as three of the ranger's fingers exploded through the wall.

"Run!" screamed Tommy. "Run!"

12

IN FOR A HOWLING GOOD TIME!

Tommy lay hidden in a small clump of trees and rocks, with cold sweat running down his face. He closed his eyes as the pain came in nauseating waves. Eevie took off her backpack. Two jagged holes, as well as two now-empty water bottles where the snake had struck, had saved her life. She crouched beside Tommy, wiping the sweat from his brow.

Tommy's eyes flicked open. He could see the worry on Eevie's face.

"You look like you got in a fight with a razor and lost," said Tommy through clenched teeth.

"Juggling chainsaws is next," said Eevie, smiling at her friend. "You're not looking so good yourself. Is...is your shoulder broken?"

"I don't think so. I think it's just dislocated."

"*Just*?" asked Eevie.

Eevie was about to ask a question when a haunting howl broke through the stillness of the forest, sending a scattering of birds screeching skyward.

Tommy jolted backwards, smacking his already aching head against his stone pillow. Eevie bolted upright, scanning their surroundings.

"Tommy...that sounded like..."

"I know what it sounded like," said Tommy, wishing he didn't.

"Tommy, we've got to find a safer place. Not to rush you, but..."

Eevie crouched down beside him. "Is there anything I can do to help with your shoulder?"

"No," he grimaced. "I'm gonna try to fix it myself."

"Do you know how to do that?"

"Maybe.... OK, not really. I once saw a kayaker put his shoulder back in place after slamming into a rock."

Ah-ooooooh.... Ah-ooooooh...

"Tommy," said Eevie panicking. "Not to rush you, but that howl seemed a lot closer."

Tommy quickly sat up as another wave of nauseating pain punched him dead in the stomach. "OK, Eevie, here goes nothing."

Sitting, Tommy slowly walked his knees back toward his chest. He raised his hands in front of the shin opposite his dislocated arm, then interlocked his fingers. The pain was so intense that he didn't think he could go through with it. Tears filled his eyes as he slowly leaned back and pushed forward with his shin. The pain was indescribable, and then...his shoulder popped back into place. His body slumped in relief as he sucked in deep breaths of air.

Eevie put her hand on Tommy's back. "You did it. You're officially as tough as a kayaker," she said, gently teasing. She sat back on her heels and roughed his hair. "I got your back," she winked kindly. Inside, Tommy had no doubts about that.

Eevie pulled her phone out of her backpack. She had expected it, but she couldn't stop the feeling of disappointment when she read "No Service" at the top. "I was going to try to geotag our location, but there's no signal," she said.

"That doesn't surprise me," said Tommy, rubbing his throbbing arm. "Who knows where we are…"

He opened his backpack and pulled out a bottle of water. Digging deeper, he pulled out a small bottle of ibuprofen. Taking a swig from the bottle, he swallowed two pills, then offered the water to Eevie.

"It's gonna be dark soon. We should find a safe place to—"

Tommy never finished his sentence. Instead he simply pointed and said, "Wolf…wolf creature!"

The wolf was massive, its luminescent white fur glowing in the darkness. It lowered its head, crouching on its muscular hind legs, growling.

Tommy scrambled to his feet, grabbing a fallen tree branch. Raising it above his head like a club, he rushed toward the wolf, screaming. Unfazed, the wolf snarled and charged. Tommy swung the branch, striking the wolf full force in the face. Crimson-red blood gushed down its snow-white snout.

"Back off, before I really get mad!" demanded Tommy, grabbing his arm. It felt like someone was wailing on his shoulder with a sledgehammer.

The wolf attacked again, leaping at Tommy, its massive jaws open wide, exposing rows of razor-sharp teeth. He kicked out furiously, catching the wolf in its soft underbelly—causing it to howl out in pain.

Tommy slowly backed away from the wolf. In a blur, the wolf charged again. Tommy stepped aside and swung the branch like a baseball bat; however, the wolf was ready this time, catching the weapon in its jaws and crushing it into pieces. Tommy looked down at his hand. All that was left was a jagged, six-inch piece of branch, which he defiantly threw at the wolf.

Suddenly, the wolf took a step back. It seemed unsure. Tommy risked a backwards glance at Eevie. She furiously stared down the wolf, her hand outstretched, the tip of her wand glowing ominously.

The wolf snarled, confused and agitated. The sight of Eevie's wand had somehow made him hesitant.

Eevie thrust the wand toward the wolf and shouted, *"Oblito Lucis!"* The wolf cowered, taking a step back. Nothing happened. *"Oblito Lucis!"* Eevie cried out again, jabbing her wand at the wolf. *Why isn't it working?*

The wolf, sensing it was in no danger, charged. "*Lucis Orbem*!" screamed Eevie. Her wand vibrated and a ball of white light surrounded the wolf's face, blinding it momentarily.

Eevie turned toward Tommy, her eyes filled with confusion and fear. "The other spells still aren't working!" she shouted. "Run!"

The trees whipped past them in a blur of browns and grays. Underbrush and roots tore at their legs and feet as they raced through the forest. Behind them they could hear the wolf closing in.

"Eevie, there's a clearing ahead. There's no way we are going to outrun that thing on flat land."

"That tree," yelled Eevie, "it's our only chance."

Tommy followed Eevie's eyes. About half a football field away was a tree that in happier times would have been the perfect treehouse tree. It sprouted big, thick branches—lots of them.

They burst from the woods into the open expanse. Eevie felt like she was running in glue; the tree never seemed to get closer. In mid-run Tommy picked up a large, jagged rock—the wolf was now in the open field gaining on them.

Tommy hesitated for just a second. When the wolf was about fifteen feet away, he hurled the rock into its face. He thought he had scored a direct hit, only to see the animal catch the rock midair and crush it in its jaws.

Tommy's attack had bought Eevie the two seconds she needed to get to safety. Running full tilt, she misjudged her footing, tripping. She slammed into the tree, knocking the wind from her lungs. Her eyes grew wide. The tree was literally on the edge of a cliff, and Tommy was running full speed toward her. If he misjudged a tiny bit...

Regaining her breath, Eevie jumped hard, and grabbed the lowest branch. She ran her feet up the tree and threw a leg over the branch. "Tommy," she screamed, "it's a cliff! Tommy!"

She grabbed another branch, pulling herself higher into the tree. She watched in horror as the wolf dove at Tommy's legs, barely missing. It rolled in a violent ball of legs and fur, and instantly was up running at Tommy again.

"Come on, Tommy, come on!" Eevie pleaded. But she knew there was no way he would make it up the tree before the wolf would reach him. "Tommy," she screamed again, "it's a cliff!"

Eevie's scream caught in her throat as she watched Tommy reach the edge of the cliff and jump—the wolf too went flying through the air. At the last second, Tommy's hands wrapped around the lowest branch. He pulled and thrusted his hips up, to swing his legs up and over the branch, but the wolf's jaw clamped down on his belt. As Tommy desperately clung to the branch, the wolf twisted and jerked wildly, trying to pull him out of the tree.

"Eevie, get my knife!" screamed Tommy. "I can't hang on!"

The weight of the wolf was too much for Tommy; his hands were slipping. Eevie raced down the tree. She had just reached his branch when a loud cracking sound pierced the air. Tommy looked up into Eevie's eyes. She watched in horror as the limb tore loose from the tree...sending Tommy and the wolf over the cliff.

"Noooo!" screamed Eevie. She raced down to the lowest branch and jumped to the ground. She ran to the edge of the cliff when suddenly, something reached up, and grabbed her by the ankle. She let out a scream as it began pulling her over the edge. "Tommy!" she exclaimed.

Literally, just below the ledge, Tommy hung, suspended by a huge root protruding from the face of the cliff. His injured arm was wrapped around the root, while his feet dangled into space. He pulled and clawed desperately with his other hand.

"Tommy, save your strength! I'll get you."

Tommy simply moaned and nodded, trying to conserve every last ounce of energy that he had to keep from falling. Eevie flung her backpack to the ground and grabbed her last coil of rope. Her hands shook violently as she raced to create a slip knot and a lasso. She leaned over the edge of the cliff and lowered it down to Tommy.

"Tommy, I'm gonna lower this lasso over you and use that to pull you up."

"OK," said Tommy hoarsely. She lowered the lasso over his head and past his arms, then slowly raised it just under his armpit.

"Tommy, I need to get the lasso completely around you. Can you switch arms?"

Tommy nodded. "I think so." He pulled up with all of his strength, which wasn't much, and twisted his torso. His left hand grabbed out into space, missing the root; a surge of panic gripped him. He hung precariously thousands of feet in the air, supported only by an injured arm.

"Come on, Tommy, come on!" screamed Eevie.

Tommy reached out. His fingertips clawed at the root, but his grip was slick with sweat. In his mind, he pictured himself falling over and over. A cold chill misted over him. He knew this attempt would be his last; he simply didn't have the strength to try again.

Swinging his body to the left, he reached out, the palm of his hand slapping against the root. He curled his fingers around it, pulled upward, and thrust his wrist and then forearm over the root. After one more hard jerk upward, the root scraped his side and locked in under his armpit.

Tommy hung his head, exhausted. Eevie worked the lasso further up his waist and under his armpit. She quickly threw the other end of the rope over the lowest branch of the tree and tied it into place.

"Tommy, I know you're tired," said Eevie breath-lessly, "but when I say go, I need you to pull with EVERYTHING you got."

Eevie sat down and braced her feet against a large root. "GO!"

She pulled with all of her might. Leaning backwards with each pull of the rope, inch by inch, the rope slowly moved forward until she could see the top of Tommy's head.

"Almost there," grunted Eevie, her eyes filled with pain as the rope mercilessly cut into her hands. Both of Tommy's forearms were now over the edge. Eevie con-tinued to pull, not wanting to let go of the rope, even for a second. Finally, Tommy's chest and stomach were on solid ground. Eevie rushed forward and grabbed his arms, Tommy grimaced in pain, as Eevie dragged him to safety.

Exhausted, they lay on the ground, staring at the sky. Eevie examined her friend, whose face and body were covered in cuts and bruises. She looked at her own hands, bloody and torn from the rope.... Had it not been for the backpack, the snake would have killed her. What had they gotten themselves into?

"I'm alive," whispered Tommy, wiggling his fingers in a celebratory exclamation punctuated by a very wimpy "yay."

"Yes, you are," said Eevie, placing her hand on his shoulder. "But, I do have a question for you. What hap-pened to your pants?"

"What?" moaned Tommy as he rolled over. Slowly, painfully, he propped himself up on his elbows.

"I never knew you were so romantic," Eevie teased.

"What?" asked Tommy, confused. His eyes followed Eevie's gesture. His shredded pants clung to the bottom of his feet, and his midsection was adorned with a pair of white boxer shorts with little red hearts.

Tommy lay his head back onto the dirt and stared up into the sky, mourning the loss of his pants and his masculinity.

13

EYE SPY A TREE!

Nighttime was coming quickly. Eevie and Tommy stared toward the sky, where millions of stars sparkled like gold glitter on black felt. A blue-white crescent moon chased a smaller, whitish-gray full moon, looking like a game of celestial Pac-Man.

Overhead, swarms of bats flew through the sky, screeching, chasing an invisible prey.

Tommy slowly walked over to the edge of the chasm and peered downward. Miles below, a small river sliced through the rock, a process that had probably taken hundreds of thousands of years.

The moment struck Tommy. The water was persistent. It created its own path, its own future—much like what they were doing: forging forward in a world they knew nothing about.

Tommy jumped at Eevie's voice. "Still contemplating cliff diving?" asked Eevie, smiling.

"Yes," Tommy paused. "I think if I jump now, I'll hit the bottom sometime tomorrow."

"Better pack a lunch," said Eevie, straight-faced. "Do you think that wolf survived?" she asked, leaning further over the edge.

"Not a chance, unless he sprouted wings," Tommy said with certainty. "But...," he paused, turning and looking across the field behind them, "...if there was one wolf, there has to be more."

"It's getting really dark..."

"I packed a tent," said Tommy, "but I think with those wolves around we would simply be a human candy bar for them."

Eevie shuddered. "I prefer not to think of myself as food."

"What about the tree?" asked Tommy. "We'd be up off the ground. I can rest some logs across those huge branches and we can spread the tent out over them."

Eevie looked at the tree. "How ironic. Last time a tree tried to kill us; this time a tree saves our lives. I am certainly conflicted at the moment as to how I feel about trees."

Tommy quickly began gathering branches and small logs while Eevie cleared a space beneath the tree, encircling it with rocks. An hour later Tommy and Eevie sat on their makeshift shelter, eating protein bars and warmed by the glow of the fire below.

All the while, they were unaware of the two eyes watching them in the darkness.

******

Eevie sat up abruptly, smacking her forehead on the branch above her head. "Why?!" she asked, annoyed. Tommy rolled over onto his shoulder and yelped in pain.

"Good morning," said Eevie, digging into her backpack. "Love your hair."

Tommy rolled his eyes and responded with an annoyed grunt.

She handed Tommy a couple of ibuprofen and a bottle of water. "I was thinking a little later you could hike down the cliff to that tiny little river and get us some fresh water."

Tommy looked up at Eevie. "Seriously? Are you trying to write a book on sarcasm? Because you are rapidly improving."

"I am, and you have the good fortune of being my guinea pig for all of my new..." Eevie stopped midsentence. The alchemy sign for death was drawn into the ashes below.

"What is it?" asked Tommy, suddenly very alert. As he looked down, a chill traveled up his spine. "The ranger...," whispered Tommy.

"Why didn't he kill us? It's like he's toying with us."

"I have no idea," said Tommy, now fully awake. "But we need to get moving."

Eevie and Tommy packed their supplies in a flash and scrambled down the tree. Eevie double checked the fire circle, making sure it was completely out.

"This stinks," he said. "We have no idea which way to go. On one side of us we have a huge cliff, and on the other side woods and more woods."

"Well, I have a suggestion," said Eevie, pointing at a series of footprints on the ground. "Let's track the ranger and see where he goes—at least that way we aren't just wandering aimlessly through the forest."

"I knew there was a reason I kept you around. Lead on."

Trekking through the forest was exhausting. Having to hyper-focus on every indentation in the dirt, and every little broken twig or misplaced plant stem, was mind-numbingly stressful.

Dozens of times, they had to backtrack through the dense undergrowth because they had missed a tiny clue that sent them in the wrong direction.

Whap! Tommy's head snapped back as Eevie flat-palmed his mouth. His lips were already forming "Wh" of "What gives" when he saw him.

Tommy froze, not daring to breathe. Just a few feet in front of them, the ranger sat on a fallen dead tree. The remains of a small, furry animal hung limp in his hand. In the stillness of the forest they could hear the crunching of bone as the ranger chewed.

"Gross," whispered Eevie in disgust.

Finished eating, the ranger stood and placed the carcass of the animal on the fallen tree. He lowered his hand over the remains and whispered, *"Exscindo."* A bright flash burst from his hand, and the carcass was gone.

"Eevie," whispered Tommy, "did you see that? He completely obliterated that thing with his hand."

Eevie nodded, blaming herself. *She couldn't even get simple spells to work; how were they supposed to fight a powerful sorcerer?*

The ranger was on the move. Stepping over the log, he began moving through the dense underbrush, traversing deeper into the shadows of the forest.

"Come on, we don't want to lose him."

"I've already lost my appetite," said Tommy, frowning. "Does that count?"

"That doesn't even make sense..."

"Says the girl following a demon creature into the forest, wearing this year's explorer's collection for middle-aged men."

Now they could see it. Barely visible, but definitely there, before them, was a narrow path cut through the forest. About an hour into the walk, the ranger suddenly stopped in front of a gnarled and twisted tree.

What at first appeared to be dark knots or burls suddenly opened, revealing dozens of eyes covering the entirety of the tree.

"Woah," exclaimed Tommy softly. He turned to Eevie. "Imagine that tree's optometrist bill."

The ranger held his hand up to the eyes and then slowly rotated it. The eyes followed his every movement. Seemingly satisfied at what they saw, they closed, vanishing into the coarse tree bark.

Touching the tree with his fingertips, the ranger spoke the word "*Resero*." Eevie and Tommy tensed, getting ready to run if necessary as the ground began to shake and the tree slowly untwisted.

"Look! There's something in the tree," breathed Eevie. She dropped to her hands and knees and crawled behind a cluster of trees to get a better view. She inched over, making room for Tommy to squeeze in beside her.

Eevie gasped at what she saw. Inside the tree was a shriveled mummy—roots and vines coiled like snakes around his body. Larger vines spread across his body, like a giant spider web pinning him to the tree. Two sunken black orbs, indentations where the eyes should be, sat above a strip of cursed paper stretched across the mummy's mouth.

"Hello, old friend," rasped the ranger, holding up a small vial of glowing blue liquid. At the site of the drink, the mummy twisted and writhed, but only succeeded in entangling himself even more.

"Why not make it easy on yourself?" growled the ranger as he reached up, ripping the cursed paper from the mummy's mouth.

"Nooo!" screamed the mummy. "Nooo!" his voice pleaded hoarsely.

The ranger grabbed the mummy's head, slamming it against the back of the tree, then covered the mummy's nose so he couldn't breathe.

Eevie and Tommy could hear the mummy's gasp for breath. They knew this was the opportunity the ranger was hoping for—and as they watched helplessly, the ranger poured the blue liquid into the mummy's mouth.

The mummy's body shuddered, and then its head fell forward, held secure in the living spider web. Satisfied, the ranger touched the tree. "*Occludo*."

The ground began to shake as the tree twisted, resealing itself, protected by the ever-watching eyes. The ranger stood still for a very long time...then quickly and deliberately turned in their direction. He was clearly listening.

Had he heard them? Tommy and Eevie held perfectly still, afraid to breathe.

The ranger reached into his pocket and pulled out what looked like a glass marble. He rested the marble on the palm of his hand and spoke. "It is done. Everything is going according to plan." He thrust the marble into his pocket and disappeared into the forest.

Wary of a trap, Eevie and Tommy remained crouched in the small grove of trees for twenty minutes before daring to move.

"You know the people that stand as still as statues for money?" asked Tommy.

"You mean like a human mannequin?"

"Yes, those! I'm marking that off my list of possible careers as soon as I get home. My legs are killing me."

"You're such a complex person, Tommy."

"It's true, I'm cursed."

"You're not cursed. Annoying yes, but not cursed. The poor guy in the tree, now he's cursed."

"Wait," said Tommy, staring at Eevie. "I know that look. You're not thinking about messing with that tree, are you? We've had some really bad luck when it comes to trees; I *don't* think this is a good idea."

"Didn't you see how much he was suffering? Are you seriously going to leave someone trapped inside a tree to die?"

Tommy glanced at the tree, measuring his next words. "Eevie, in all seriousness, that tree...," he pointed at it, "...is possessed, and we have no idea what will happen if we go near it."

"We have to try, Tommy. Whoever that is, is obviously an enemy of the ranger. He may be able to help us—or at least provide some answers. Or...," she paused, "...we continue to follow the ranger through the woods, and hope he doesn't realize we're shadowing him."

Tommy shook his head. "I don't like this idea at all..."

"I know, me neither, but we have limited options."

"What if those eyes open? What if they are like some kind of—I don't know—early warning system? If they see two kids standing there, I'm sure it's gonna alert someone, somewhere that we don't want to meet."

"Tommy, we just need to think everything through. We can't just wing through this one."

"Winging it last time nearly got you skewered. I wonder if Amazon has a return policy on backpacks damaged by snake bites."

"Oh my God! You really do have problems focusing. Your mind must be like a kaleidoscope on sugar."

"You have no idea."

"OK...can you please figure this out? We just need to go through what the ranger did."

"All right," agreed Tommy.

"First, he approached the tree," said Eevie, replaying the scene in her head.

"Then those creepy eyes opened," Tommy added, "and he did that weird British queen wave, where he showed the front and back of his hand."

"That's right!" Eevie nodded her head in agreement. "And then he said something that sounded like 'raise arrow,' which I'm sure is a spell." Eevie pulled her phone out, tapped on the screen, navigated to images, and began to scroll through the pictures she had taken of the spell book.

"*Resero*," said Eevie excitedly. "*Resero* means open."

"And then he said something that sounded like 'Oh Pluto' to close the tree."

Eevie quickly swiped across the screen. "*Occludo* means to close!"

"Awesome, so...that's everything except it doesn't solve the problem with those creepy eyes seeing two kids."

"That part is easy," said Eevie, removing her backpack and producing a roll of duct tape.

"You are not going to wrap me up like a mummy," Tommy said.

"No...but I must admit the idea does sound tempting," Eevie said with smile. "OK, we just need to make sure our faces are completely covered. Pull your hoodie down. I'm gonna use the duct tape and make sure everything is covered except a tiny slit for your eyes."

Tommy pulled the hoodie over his face, bunching up the material so that only a tiny black gap was visible for his eyes. Eevie placed a couple pieces of tape to hold everything in place. She took a step back. "I can't see your eyes. Can you see?"

"Yeah," answered Tommy's muffled voice. "I have no peripheral vision, but I can see."

Tommy helped Eevie adjust and secure her hood. "You're right!" she exclaimed. "I can only see what's directly in front of me."

"After the eyes close, we should be OK," Tommy said. "We should be able to take off our hoods then."

Eevie didn't answer. She was already feeling her way into the opening, walking slowly toward the tree.

14

IF YOU'RE FEELING FROGGY!

"Eevie, wait!" implored Tommy, as they approached the tree. The ground beneath their feet began to tremble and the roots twisted and undulated, making it difficult to stand. Suddenly, hundreds of eyes opened simultaneously. The effect was overwhelming, paralyzing Eevie and Tommy with fear.

Eevie felt a strange tug in her right hand. *That's right,* she remembered, raising her hand to the tree.

"Argh!" She screamed out in pain. *Something wasn't right.* She tried to tear her eyes away, but she couldn't. Against her will, her wand suddenly appeared in her hand. She fought desperately as an invisible force tried to rip it from her grasp.

"Eevie!" screamed Tommy, bewildered. "Eevie!"

Tommy stepped in front of her, blocking her view of the tree. The roots began wrapping around their ankles. As Tommy held up his hand to the tree, a strange sensation ran up his hand through his ring finger. The eyes of the serpent ring that encircled his finger opened. Tommy watched as the eyes stared at his ring.

"She's with *me*!" Tommy hissed. "Let her be!"

Tommy felt the roots go slack around his ankles, and then the eyes snapped shut. Eevie staggered backwards, rubbing her throbbing hand.

"What just happened?" inquired Eevie, confused.

"I think it's because of this ring," said Tommy, holding up his hand. "The ranger has the same ring...that's what he was showing the tree."

"It was trying to get my wand, and I couldn't stop it, and then...I didn't want to stop it."

"It's OK," Tommy assured. "We're here together. We're a team." He took a deep breath. "Somehow those eyes put you in a trance.... We're dealing with magic and powers we don't understand. We're gonna have to be careful."

"We better open this tree before those eyes open again," Eevie said. "Not sure the ring will work twice."

"Do you want me to do the honors?" asked Tommy nodding at the tree.

"You better.... You have the exclusive members-only ring that gets you into all of the meet-and-greets."

"OK, what was the word he said again?" asked Tommy.

"*Resero*," Eevie whispered quietly, weary of awakening the tree again.

Tommy slowly placed his fingertips on the tree. He could feel energy gently coursing through him. "*Resero*." Tommy spoke the word gently, but firmly.

He and Eevie stepped back as the tree untwisted, groaned, and opened. The rough sound of bark and roots uncoiling sounded like thunder in the solitude of the forest. The smell emanating from the tree was sickening and pungent like something had died. Tightly ensnared inside the belly of the tree, the mummy's body hung limp, like a marionette waiting to be controlled by its master.

Up close they could see that instead of cloth, the mummy was completely entombed by thousands of vines and small branches. Across his mouth, the ranger had reattached a white strip of paper, with some type of unidentifiable writing.

"What is that paper across his mouth? Do you think it's safe to touch?" asked Tommy, hesitating.

"I think that is some type of prayer seal, like if a certain area is demon-possessed, priests used these seals to keep away the evil spirits. According to some religions, King Solomon was given a special seal that enabled him to command demons and speak to animals."

"Wait, so is this seal keeping him from being possessed by evil spirits, or is the prayer thingy preventing evil spirits from escaping from him?"

"I don't know," said Eevie worriedly. "I just know what I've read."

"OK, thank you for the history lesson," said Tommy. "Now, prepare to run if necessary."

Eevie nodded, her eyes glued to the mummy.

He reached up and carefully pulled the seal from the mummy's mouth. Hot, disgusting breath rushed out from its mouth, as if it had been holding it for centuries. The mummy moaned and slowly attempted to right its head.

"Help me...," breathed the mummy.

"Who are you?" asked Eevie. "Who did this to you?"

"Sorceress, evil sorceress." The mummy's voice was feeble and weak. "Please help me."

"How?" asked Tommy.

"The adamas flower's nectar."

"Adamas flower?" asked Eevie, confused.

"Yes, the diamond flower. This and the tears of the moonbow frog."

Tommy looked at Eevie and arched his eyebrows. "I think the ranger may have given him a little too much of that blue stuff."

"It's the antidote to counteract the spell. You must hurry," rasped the mummy.

"We're gonna help you, but we don't have any idea where to find the adamas flower or the frog."

"There is a small river...half mile north from here," the mummy said in his weakened voice. "The adamas flower grows just on the edge of the water. They are very hard to see as they are crystal clear, like glass."

The mummy coughed from deep in his lungs, his breathing becoming more labored. "You'll find the flower there. Pull the flower from the stem. Inside the flower you will see a long white string. The end will have a drop of nectar on it."

"And the frog?" asked Tommy, biting his lip painfully, feeling like this was all a bad dream.

"The moonbow frog hides under rocks and logs. He's easily distinguishable because his skin is blue and yellow, like the moon. Once the frog ingests the fluid, his eyes will cry a green liquid. That liquid will counteract my poison."

"Is he poisonous?" asked Eevie.

"Only if you lick him," said the mummy.

Tommy interrupted. "Just so we're clear: You want us to find a diamond flower, get its nectar, make a frog eat it, and then collect the green tears that come from its eyes, and then feed the tears to you?"

"Yes," whispered the mummy.

Tommy turned to Eevie, a flabbergasted look on his face. "And I was hoping it was going to be something challenging."

"Is there anything else we need to know?" asked Eevie.

"Yes, please hur..."

"Please hurry, we know.... Come on, Eevie."

Eevie gave Tommy an exasperated look and shook her head. Her eyes told him that she was not happy with him. She pulled her phone from her jeans and swiped her finger across the screen.

"Darn, I can't geotag our location."

"Oh, you're kidding me," said Tommy in mock surprise. "You mean Google doesn't have a 'choose your quest' option, with maps and alternate routes?"

Eevie ignored him and opened her virtual compass. "North is that way," she said, pointing. "Let's go."

A half mile of trekking through dense undergrowth was slow and tiring. Thorny green bushes tore at their clothing and skin, and incredibly strong spaghetti-like vines continuously coiled around their feet, tripping them.

"I feel like the freaking pied piper of plants," said Tommy, hacking away with his knife at a particularly amorous vine that had wrapped possessively around his waist, refusing to let go.

"You are so dramatic," laughed Eevie. "You fight a massive snake and a wolf, and now you're crying 'uncle' because of a little vegetation?"

"Yeah, well you saw what a *little*...," Tommy raised his hand in air quotes, emphasizing *little*, "...vegetation did to mummy man. He looks like a talking shrub."

"Shhh, listen," said Eevie, splaying her hand across Tommy's face.

Tommy nodded. The sound of water splashing over rocks greeted them. "Perfect," he said. "Let's go find some flowers and frogs."

The mummy was right. Within a few minutes of wading in freezing water, Eevie was able to find several adamas flowers. She was careful to remove the entire flower including its roots. She hated destroying such a beautiful flower; its petals glistened like wet crystal.

Tommy was not so lucky. He found everything except the moonbow frog. "What if this thing..." *Splash!* Tommy turned his face as he flipped over another rock, "...doesn't even exist?"

"Why would the mummy lie to us? He's obviously in pain, and I'm pretty sure he doesn't want to live in a tree..."

"He could be hallucinating. Who knows what the ranger..." *Splash* "...gave him? I've turned over a hundred rocks and found nothing but weird slug creatures and a couple of snakes."

"Didn't he say logs too?" asked Eevie.

Tommy warily looked up the riverbed. He despised the thought of trudging through the forest again, looking under decaying logs. After lifting enough logs to build a modest home, he finally uncovered the evasive moonbow frog.

"Yes, found you!" Tommy exclaimed excitedly. The frog was stunning. The blues and yellows were so vibrant that they looked unreal. The spectacular amphibian was much larger than he expected, about the size and shape of an avocado sliced down the middle.

Without moving his eyes from the frog, Tommy carefully took off his backpack, reached inside, and grabbed a shirt. He crouched, then dove toward the frog, trapping it.

"Got him!" yelled Tommy. "I got him."

Eevie rushed over to Tommy, placing the adamas flowers on the ground. She selected the healthiest looking specimen from the bunch.

Tommy crouched once again, grabbing a water bottle and duct tape from his backpack. Eevie looked at him, a confused expression on her face.

"We don't have any place to put the tear drops, so I'm gonna catch them in this," said Tommy, holding up the bottle top. "Then I'll seal it with a piece of duct tape."

"I'm impressed...," said Eevie.

"Eevie, when you look at me, you should *expect* greatness. *Surprise* simply tells me you doubt my ability to succeed."

"I'm at a loss for words..."

"Again, it's being in the presence of..."

"Oh my God, Tommy, just grab the frog!"

Tommy startled and then reluctantly picked up the frog. Immediately, a pungent odor filled the air.

"Tommy!" yelled Eevie. "Why?"

"It wasn't me," said Tommy, looking incredulously at Eevie. "It was the frog!"

Disgust crossed both of their faces as a huge wet spot appeared, soaking through the fabric of Tommy's shirt.

"And...that would be the poison he was talking about," said Eevie matter-of-factly.

"Great," said Tommy as he rotated the frog so they were eye to eye. Eevie carefully pinched off the top of the flower from the stem. Sure enough, a sticky white string dangled from the base of the flower. Eevie slowly and gently pulled. The string broke free from the flower, and at the end, a single drop of nectar glistened.

The frog's eyes grew twice their normal size, as he stared hungrily at the drop of nectar. Tommy moved the frog toward Eevie's hand, but before he could blink, the frog's tongue flicked out and grabbed the drop of nectar, sucking it into its mouth.

"Woah...that was impressive," said Tommy. The frog became very still. Immediately, dark green liquid began flowing from its eyes.

Tommy placed the cap under the frog's eye, capturing as much of the liquid as possible. He gently sat the frog down where he had found him. They had succeeded in filling the bottle cap halfway.

"I hope that's enough to cure the mummy," Eevie said.

"I bet you never thought you'd say those words," laughed Tommy.

"It's a person trapped inside all of those roots and branches—we can't just leave him."

"I know," said Tommy, placing a small piece of duct tape securely across the top of the cap. "Right now, I just want to wash the poison off my hands and get moving before it's dark. We've been out here for hours."

They headed back to see the mummy. After Tommy face-planted twice, a victim of more amorous vegetation, Eevie was assigned the honor of entrusted bottle cap carrier.

They suffered for what seemed hours, enduring what could only be described as *plant abuse*, before they arrived at the tree. Both the mummy and tree were just how they had left them.

"He looks comfy." The mummy appeared startled upon hearing Tommy's voice.

"Did you get the antidote?" the mummy rasped.

"We did," said Eevie as she cautiously removed the tape from the bottle cap, careful not to spill a single drop. She placed her hand on the mummy's shoulder, steadying herself, as she pulled at the vines covering his mouth.

"OK, I'm going to attempt to get this in your mouth," she said, her calmness betrayed by the quiver in her voice. She touched the cap to where she thought his lips would be, and poured until more than half of the liquid was gone.

Eevie stepped back from the tree, not knowing what to expect. Immediately, the vines began to turn black, then fall away. Before them stood what could only be described as a living skeleton. His hairless, white skin was so thin and dry that it seemed impossible that it could contain the bones encased within without tearing. It was inconceivable that this man could still be alive.

He slowly opened his eyes, his pupils abnormally large and black, and whispered, "More."

There was nothing in Eevie's mind to prepare her for this. She had never seen another human being this close to death, so horrifically emaciated. Numbly, she stepped forward, moved the cap to his lips once again, and poured a tiny rivulet of antidote, which glistened like a green emerald in the corner of his pale, cracked lips.

"Thank you," breathed the withered man.

"You're welcome," said Eevie, kindly. "May I ask your name?"

"Vayne," he said simply, not inquiring the same of Eevie and Tommy.

"You said a sorceress did this to you. Who is she? Does the man who gave you the potion earlier today work for her?"

The man hesitated before answering, then looked directly into Eevie's eyes. "You will soon find there is an evil here...an evil that cannot be destroyed. Many have tried, like me, but she is too powerful. She has destroyed all who oppose her in this world, and now...she will destroy your world."

"Has anyone here considered anger management?" Tommy asked. "There is so much hostility? Maybe some mindfulness? Meditation...?"

Eevie glared at Tommy.

"What?" he asked with a bewildered look on his face. "It has its merits."

Eevie turned her attention back to Vayne. "What about the man—the man who gave you the potion earlier?" she inquired. "Who is he?"

"Maleficum." The man spat out his name in disgust. "He is an assassin, the most evil of demons. Thousands have died at his hands...thousands."

Ranger Rick has killed thousands of people? Tommy mused to himself. *Who knew? He seems like such a nice guy.*

As the man spoke, he began to transform. A few vines still clung to his arms and to his body, but it was obvious they were weakening. Black striations began to appear in the roots and vines, like bruised veins. Dark hair began to grow on the man's head, and his body began to change, becoming muscular and vibrant.

Within minutes the man had transformed from a skeleton into a healthy-looking man in his late thirties. A smile stretched across his face, as he sucked deep breaths into his lungs. He looked down at his hands, opening and closing them, obviously pleased at his metamorphosis.

"There seems to be a little magic left in these vines," he said, working to free his arms. His voice surprised Tommy. It was now strong and even. "Can you help break me free?"

"Uhm... sure," said Tommy, apprehensively. Something inside his stomach told him this was a bad idea.

Eevie and Tommy pulled at the last remaining vines that imprisoned him. The man's eyes dropped to Tommy's hand. "That's an interesting ring," he said, smiling.

A strange chill ran through Tommy. "A friend gave it to me."

"I see..."

Tommy's heart began to pound in his temples. He knew that the man didn't believe him.

"Eevie, I think it's time we get back to..."

Vayne interrupted Tommy midsentence. "You want to know why the sorceress's evil can never be destroyed?" He didn't wait for an answer. His face filled with a horrific grin. "Because I *kill* everyone who tries to stop her."

Vayne ripped free from the tree, brutally grabbing Eevie by the neck. With superhuman strength, he began crushing her throat. Tommy reached into his belt, grabbing his knife, then thrust it into the man's side.

Cold black blood rushed down searing Tommy's hand. The man screamed and lashed out with his arm, catching Tommy hard across his face. The salty taste of blood filled Tommy's mouth.

Eevie viciously kicked Vayne in the stomach. He lost his footing and crashed backwards into the tree.

"*Occludo!*" screamed Tommy. "*Occludo!*"

Vayne screamed as the tree began closing around him. Tommy and Eevie raced away toward the forest.

Seconds later, a powerful scream ripped through the air as Vayne literally exploded from the tree. In a flash, he was gaining on them.

"Wand!" The wand suddenly appeared in Eevie's hand, vibrating and ready for action.

Surprise filled the man's face, and he quickly darted behind a tree for cover. Eevie screamed the spell she had heard the ranger use to vaporize the remains of the animal he'd eaten. "*Exscindo*!"

Nothing happened. "*Exscindo*!" she said more forcefully. She stared at her hand in disbelief. "Awe, come on! Tommy, nothing is working!" cried Eevie.

Sneering, the man stepped out from behind the tree. "Poor human," he laughed. "I'm going to tear that wand from your hand!" His words both frightened and angered Eevie.

She whirled again, facing Vayne, and screamed, "*Expelliarmus*!" A bush next to Tommy exploded, raining down bits of rock and roots onto him.

"What are you doing?" yelled Tommy as he covered his head. "This isn't Harry Potter—this is real life, Eevie! You're gonna get us killed!"

"Sorry, we can't outrun him, Tommy. He's way too fast."

"Eevie, I have a plan," said Tommy between breaths as they raced through the forest. "That huge rock," he said, pointing ahead. "Take this." He tore off his hoodie and backpack and handed them to her. "Prop my hoodie up, so it looks like I'm hiding with you."

"Got it!" said Eevie as she grabbed the balled-up hoodie.

"He'll come to you," Tommy said. "When he does, I need you to do the illumination spell to distract him. Aim at his face! I'll have a special surprise for him."

Eevie tore off through the woods. She slid behind the rock, just as Vayne came into view. Taking a stick, she put it in the hood of Tommy's hoodie and raised it just enough for it to be visible as he approached. Using the stick, she moved it like a puppeteer.

Eevie could hear the man approaching. She fought to control her breathing and to calm herself. She whispered the word "wand," closed her eyes for a brief second, and then whispered a self-reassuring "thank you."

Crouching, she used the stone to pull herself up onto the balls of her feet. She could hear Vayne's breathing and the crackling of dry leaves and sticks as he approached. *Where is Tommy? I hope he's ready!*

"Oh, I wonder where they are," laughed Vayne as he approached the rock. "I know you don't know how to work your wand, little girl." He spoke evilly.

Eevie jumped up and screamed, *"Lucis Orbem!"* The man sneered and merely swatted her spell aside like an annoying insect.

"Is that the best you've got? An illumination spell?" His voice dripped with disdain.

"We freed you. Why are you after us?" asked Eevie earnestly. "We could have let you die!"

"Tsk, tsk.... Your friend tried to warn you. Seems like he's the *better* judge of character," Vayne smiled, cruelly taunting her. "And where is that brave little boy who sends you out to battle? Cowering behind the rock?" Vayne laughed patronizingly. "No matter." His smile turned evil as he raised his hand toward Eevie.

"You see, I don't need a wand." He paused, clearly enjoying the moment. "You had your turn—now it's my turn.... *Voski...*"

Vayne never got a chance to finish his curse. He did, however, meet the full impact of Tommy's body weight, as he came crashing down from the tree above, slamming onto Vayne's head and shoulders. Vayne's body collapsed to the ground in a heap.

"I may not know magic, but I know gravity," smiled Tommy.

Tommy quickly jumped to his feet. "Eevie, help me! Get the rope from my backpack."

While Eevie grabbed the rope, Tommy hooked his hands under Vayne's armpits and dragged him to a small tree. Quickly she looped the rope around him several times; then, pulling it tight, she secured him to the tree.

"Enjoy your stay...we know how much you like trees," Eevie said condescendingly, patting him on the head.

It wasn't thirty seconds later as they ran through the forest that they heard an angry scream, followed by a flash of light.

"I'm guessing that was a 'break free from the ropes' spell," puffed Eevie as she dodged trees and roots. "Probably not a good thing."

"Neither is that," said Tommy, pointing at the clearing that lay just ahead of them.

"We can stick along the outside perimeter of the forest so we're not as visible. Which way should we go?" asked Eevie.

"Let's go left." Tommy looked at Eevie, who seemed to expect an explanation. "It just feels right."

They ran quickly, hugging the shadows that extended just beyond the edge of the forest. *Slam!* Simultaneously they both fell to the ground.

"Ugh," moaned Eevie, who slowly sat up.

Tommy was on his hands and knees, rubbing his forehead. "What happened?"

"Hurry, hurry! Get inside!" a woman's voice urgently beckoned.

Tommy looked at Eevie. "You heard that, right?" he said.

Suddenly a woman's arm and face appeared, hovering in space above them.

"Hurry, come inside or you'll be seen! Now, or he will kill you!" she demanded.

Eevie and Tommy stepped into nothingness, via an invisible door.

15

THE SNAKE IS HISS-TORY!

Eevie and Tommy stood inside a small cabin. From where they stood they could see a kitchen, a hallway, and a study filled with books and all types of glass cylinders and vials. The house smelled like gingerbread and coffee. For the moment, they felt safe.

"Thank you," stammered Eevie, confused and disoriented. "What just happened?"

"I'm Cassara, and I'm pretty sure that my ex-husband fooled you two into setting him free from his imprisonment."

"The mummy is your ex-husband?" stammered Eevie.

"Yes, Vayne tried to poison me when I wouldn't swear my allegiance to Severin."

"Sorry about that," said Tommy quietly. "We saw Maleficum giving him a potion...we thought he was a good guy."

Cassara smiled at Tommy. "It's hard to know who to trust," she said. Cassara wore her blondish brown hair pulled into a tight ponytail, revealing a kind face and intelligent eyes that gave the appearance of someone who had seen too much.

Eevie felt an immediate connection. Cassara moved with efficiency and authority, the traits of a person who knows how to get things done.

Cassara paused for a moment as if deep in thought. "I don't mean to be impolite, but we haven't much time," she said. She turned and placed her hand on the wall. Instantly the wall became transparent, enabling them to see the forest and the field.

"Now quickly, tell me who you are and why you are here."

Eevie introduced herself and Tommy. She quickly told her about the clues her grandfather had left for her and what she had found. She showed Cassara the book, and told her how they had used the astrolabe to solve the code and decrypt the spells. And when Eevie whispered the word "wand," tears slowly fell from Cassara's eyes.

"Finally," whispered Cassara, touching Eevie's shoulder. "Finally, there's hope."

"May I please ask a question about the wand?"

No longer speaking, Cassara stared intently at Tommy's hand. He lifted his hand and, suddenly, the serpent's eyes opened!

"Who gave you that ring?!" asked Cassara, spitting out the words.

"No one!" said Tommy, jumping back from her accusatory stare.

"What do you mean no one?" she said, jerking Tommy by the arm, pulling him into the room with potions and vials.

"Hey!" said Tommy, confused. "What are you doing?"

A twisted wand made of silver and gold sprang from Cassara's hand. She held it to the hollow of Tommy's throat. "Why do you have the ring of the dark sorceress?"

"Woah," said Tommy, pulling his arm free. "No one gave me this ring. I got this stupid ring trying to rescue me and Eevie from an underground labyrinth. If you didn't solve the riddles, you would die. I stupidly put my finger in a hole thinking there was a lever or some kind of button, and instead..." Tommy paused and looked at his finger, "...I've been cursed with this thing ever since."

"I tried to destroy it," spoke up Eevie. "I had one as well. When it came into contact with my wand, it was destroyed. I tried using my wand on Tommy's ring, but nothing happened."

"Cassara, what's going on?" pleaded Tommy, urgently.

"It's a tracker," whispered Cassara. "The eyes are the eyes of the sorceress...and now...she knows that I'm alive."

Tommy's heart broke. Tears poured down his cheeks. "I'm so sorry. I didn't know."

"I know you didn't." Cassara's face grew firm. "We need to destroy this ring."

Cassara led Tommy over to a wooden table filled with assorted jars and bottles. She stretched his arm across the table, turning his palm face down. Instantly, sweat covered Tommy's forehead, and his mouth went dry.

"Eevie," commanded Cassara, "hold his hand still. No matter what, don't let him move."

"Tommy," Cassara said, her jaw set tight. "This is going to hurt."

Tommy nodded, knowing there was no other choice. He closed his eyes and tried to focus on his breathing. His body trembled in anticipation of the pain about to come. Eevie watched as Cassara dipped a small dagger into one vial and then another, coating the surface of the blade. She then pointed to a black candle and whispered, "*Accendo*." A flame suddenly appeared.

Cassara thrust the knife into the flame, and instantly the blade became white hot. She nodded at Eevie. "Hold tight."

Tommy clenched his jaw and squeezed his eyes shut. Suddenly his brain exploded in pain. He screamed as Cassara placed the white-hot dagger onto the serpent ring and whispered, "*Uro*."

The head of the snake raised up in agony and attempted to bury its head into the flesh of Tommy's finger.

Tommy's screams became whimpers, as pain tore through his nerves like shards of broken glass, ripping and tearing their way to his brain. The snake's body writhed and twisted once more and then turned to ash. Tommy's hand slipped through Eevie's as he slumped onto the floor, unconscious. A low rumble that sounded like thunder shook the small house. Cassara's eyes widened in alarm.

Eevie rushed over to Tommy and cradled his head in her arms. His finger was blistered and disfigured.

"What have you done?!" Eevie cried out. "He's in agony! You've destroyed his finger!"

Cassara ignored her, then quickly mixed the contents of different vials and tubes. Another thunderous boom shook the table, causing the jars and vials to rattle.

"What is that sound?" asked Eevie, afraid she already knew the answer.

Cassara remained silent, focusing on her task at hand. She hurried over to Tommy. Gently opening his jaw, she poured the contents of the potion she had just created into his mouth.

She touched Tommy's finger and whispered, "*Glacio velocitas.*" Instantly, Tommy's finger became protected in a thin coating of ice.

Cassara turned to Eevie. "I need you to listen to me. I gave him a powerful healing herb and pain reliever. He'll be much better in a matter of minutes.... The sound that you hear is Vayne. He's casting spells to find out where you are. My suspicions are he knows that I have found you and that I'm helping you."

"Thank you," whispered Eevie. "I'm so sorry I yelled at you."

"I would have been surprised if you hadn't. Eevie, I'm afraid we only have a matter of minutes before Vayne finds us." She touched the wall. The bookshelves vanished, and Eevie could now see him, about fifty yards from the house, closing in.

"He can't see us, right? And the house is protected by spells—he can't get in, right?"

"No, he can't see us, but he'll find the house...he knows it's here. He's a very powerful and dangerous sorcerer. He was weakened by my spell, but with every minute that passes, he'll grow stronger. My protection spells won't keep him out for long."

Boom! A much stronger explosion rocked the house. Books rained down from their shelves, and pictures crashed to the floor.

Tommy sat up and rested his head against the wall.

"Is it storming?" he asked, still disoriented.

Eevie started to reply, but thought best to give him a few seconds to recover.

Tommy raised his hand and stared at his finger. He breathed in, fighting back the raw emotion that filled his chest.

"I never thought I would be free from that thing." His voice caught in his throat. "Thank you," he whispered.

Cassara nodded at him and smiled. "You're welcome. It's a small favor."

The house shook with such ferocity that it felt like it was literally being torn from the ground and hurled into space. Tommy scrambled backwards, jabbing his hand at the transparent wall.

"Vayne! It's Vayne—he's right there!" Tommy exclaimed.

Vayne stood in the field, his hand outstretched as if feeling the air around him. He now stared directly at the house, a wicked grin forming on his face.

"He's found us," gasped Eevie.

"Children, look!" Cassara hurriedly pulled out a small golden locket from around her neck. She opened it, revealing a small, polished golden stone.

"Listen carefully!" she commanded. "Behind this house you will see two white oaks. Run between those trees until you reach a stream. When you reach the stream, drop this stone into the water. *Do not move!* My friend will be there to help get you to safety."

An incredible blast struck the house. The side wall caved inward, slamming them to the floor.

"Cassara," cried Eevie, "we'll stay and help you!"

"No!" yelled Cassara. "You MUST escape! I can hold him off for a while. Hurry!"

Tommy tried to protest. Cassara looked at him sadly, raised her hand, and breathed, "*Exmoveo*."

"No!" screamed Tommy, throwing out his arms toward her.

Suddenly they were ripped backwards into a swirling vortex, and the next instance they were in the woods. Turning 360, all they could see was trees and more trees. The house had vanished. There was nothing they could do now but find the stream and follow Cassara's command.

"She's going to die trying to save us," said Eevie, choking on her words.

Tommy turned to Eevie. "Let's not discredit Cassara. She's a powerful sorceress herself. We have to have faith in her abilities. Remember, she's beaten Vayne before. We're here for a reason...and now, we need to find her friend quickly, before Vayne realizes we've escaped."

Eevie nodded. With a determined look on her face, she said, "Let's go!"

16

TOMMY NEARLY BECOMES THE SECRET IN-GREDIENT IN PAUL'S STEW

Just as Cassara had described, two majestic white oaks stood like centurions guarding the way into the forest. Tommy and Eevie quickly scanned the perimeter. There were no other white oaks.

They ran between the two trees, into the forest. Immediately the temperature dropped, and like a pair of hands closing in around a moth, the forest closed in around them. The trees and plants took on a gray, gloomy appearance.

"Eeesh, this is dismal," said Eevie as they hurried through underbrush and trees.

Splash! Suddenly, Eevie and Tommy found themselves on their hands and knees in a shallow stream. There was no lush vegetation on the bank, no clear warning that there may be water ahead. The stream simply sliced through the middle of the forest.

"Found the stream," said Tommy as he climbed onto dry land, giving Eevie his hand to help pull her back onto the shore.

"OK," said Eevie, wringing off her hands and wiping them on her jeans. "I guess this is the stream Cassara told us about."

A strong, cold wind raced through the forest, sending a chill up their spines. The wind turned and whipped back toward them. Eevie pulled her hair from her face and mouth. Her eyes were open wide.

"It's Vayne—he's searching for us...," said Eevie, as a look of sad realization filled her face. "He must have defeated Cassara."

Tommy shook his head. "Cassara was too smart—I'm sure she got away." But Tommy knew that Cassara wouldn't risk the chance of Vayne escaping...she would never let him come after them if she were still alive.

Eevie pulled out the golden stone. It felt warm in her hand from being in her pocket. "Thank you, Cassara," she whispered as it fell like a tear from her hand into the water.

A light fog drifted above the water, and then the water hardened into what looked like a giant sheet of ice. Eevie crouched and leaned forward onto her hands. Her reflection stared back at her. Suddenly, from beneath the icy surface a face appeared. Eevie gasped, surprised, and sat back on her heels. There was something oddly familiar in the crystal blue eyes, the shape of the face. A white wispy beard swirled around his chin like a storm cloud, gently moving with the water's current.

He stared intently at Eevie for a moment, and then his face relaxed into a smile.

Tommy leaned over Eevie's shoulder and whispered, "Tell him Cassara sent us."

Eevie nodded. "I know, I know.... Sir," said Eevie awkwardly, "Cassara sent us. Vayne is free, she said to find you."

A look of concern flashed across the man's face.

"Children...," his voice was commanding but calming, "...stay where you are. I will be there in a moment to guide you to safety. *Stay where you are!*"

Another powerful gust of wind blew through the forest, rippling the waters, causing the man's face to diffuse, as if it were melting. Just as before, the wind turned and raced back across them.

Just as suddenly as it had appeared, the face in the water vanished. Tommy and Eevie looked at each other as they sat by the edge of the water. The crystal layer of ice dissolved into a misty cloud, and the water returned to normal. At the bottom of the stream, Eevie could see Cassara's rock. She reached into the cold water, retrieving the stone. She stared at it for a moment, then placed it in her pocket, a reminder of their friend's bravery and sacrifice.

"Children!" His voice nearly made them jump out of their skins. "This way," the old man beckoned, motioning with his hands.

Tommy and Eevie quickly followed. The old man wasn't wasting any time—he was already hurrying away from them into the forest.

"Quickly," his voice called out, filled with urgency. "We only have moments before Vayne arrives!"

They followed in silence. Gradually the terrain changed from dense forest to rocky crags dotted with thick vertical patches of spiny vegetation, which resembled a bushel of green variegated sword blades pointing skyward. Both Eevie and Tommy fought desperately not to touch them as they slipped and slid behind the old man, who proved to be as agile as a mountain goat.

Ahead they could hear the crashing and splashing of water hitting the rocks. The old man paused and turned toward them. "Stay close—we're almost there."

Seconds later, they arrived at a huge stone cliff face, guarded by a monstrous rock. The pathway seemed impassible, but the old man began climbing up the rock. From Tommy and Eevie's angle, you could not see it, but hidden steps had been carved into the rock, and were only visible from a specific angle.

"Woah, this is cool—invisible steps," whispered Tommy.

Eevie nodded. She focused on hand and foot placement as she climbed the rock, just behind the mysterious man. The steps led them up and over the gigantic rock, depositing them just a few feet away from a massive waterfall.

Tommy looked up at the powerful waterfall. *We'll be crushed.* "I hope you don't expect us to..."

"*Indespectus disseptum*," commanded the old man as he raised his hand toward the waterfall. Instantly, a dark, narrow passageway opened through the center.

Eevie and Tommy paused, dumbstruck.

"Follow me," said the old man as he turned toward them. A small smile played across his lips; he seemed amused by their expressions.

As soon as they were safely through, the waterfall thundered, and a wall of rock closed behind them, concealing the entrance to the man's home.

It took a moment for their eyes to adjust, then they found themselves inside a huge, cathedral-shaped room. A network of candle-lit hallways extended outward, like spokes of a wheel. The man touched the wall behind the waterfall, and it instantly became transparent.

The pie-shaped room was divided into three rooms, and each section seemed to have a very specific purpose. There was a kitchen, a study, and a room very similar to Cassara's workroom, filled with glass cylinders, test tubes, books, and charts.

A large fireplace squatted like a stone giant against a wall in the kitchen. And directly in front of the fireplace stood a small, hairless creature, who looked like an elf dressed in canvas overalls.

Eevie glanced at Tommy as if to say, *Do you see him?* Then she looked back toward the creature, mesmerized as he slowly stirred a steaming pot, filled with some sort of bubbly ooze that smelled like burning black licorice.

"Ah, I see that you've noticed my friend Paullum," said the old man, gesturing.

The creature turned and looked down its long, narrow nose at the old man with a *You have got to be kidding me* expression spread across his face.

The man nodded toward Paullum, acknowledging his discontent. "Paullum goes by Paul. You see, in Latin Paullum means tiny or miniscule, and he believes that this name belittles the raw power he clearly exudes."

Tommy snickered. He tried to stop himself, but his lips quivered and then his mouth betrayed him. "And he thinks the name Paul exemplifies raw power?" he asked.

"Come here, human boy," said the tiny creature, his voice thin and raspy.

Paul threw his wooden ladle into the pot, splashing boiling black goo onto his canvas overalls. He looked at the liquid dripping down his chest and then at Tommy, his oversized eyes boiling over with anger.

Tommy's eyes grew wide as the little creature's long fingers turned blood red and began pulsing like a ticking time bomb.

"Woah!" said Tommy, taking a step back and holding out his hands. "You exude power! OK?! You exude! Jeesh, someone needs anger management," whispered Tommy, looking from Eevie to the old man for affirmation.

"That does it, human boy," the tiny creature growled. "I can hear you." Paul jabbed his red pulsating finger at his own ear, which Tommy realized had grown twice in size. "Let's see how you like..."

"Paul!" said the man sternly. He was smiling, but his expression said *cool it*. "These are guests, *special* guests. I am quite sure they respect you and *all* of your unique and incredibly powerful gifts."

Paul paused as if deep in thought, and then relented with a "Hmph, we'll see about that."

He nodded curtly to Eevie and Tommy, turned, and with a snap of his fingers, the wooden ladle was back in his hand. He hummed quietly to himself as he stirred the frothy brew. Tommy noticed, however, that his ear was still twice its normal size, which meant he was going to listen to every word they said.

"Now," said the man as he turned his attention to Eevie and Tommy. "I can see on your faces that you must have a lot of questions for me, and I too have a lot of questions for you. How about the easy part first," he said kindly. "I'm Charles—Charles Dixon."

Eevie smiled. "I'm Eevie Davenport."

"And I'm Thomas Prescott." Tommy could see Paul moving his head back and forth, mimicking him as he said his name.

Eevie turned and looked at her friend, knotting her eyebrows. "Thomas?" she asked questioningly. "His name is Tommy. Everyone calls him Tommy," said Eevie.

"Tommeee," snickered Paul. "Tommy, avenger of the dead, soldier of doom, Tommeee..."

"It's an honor to meet you," smiled Charles. He looked at Paul and shook his head. "He only picks on the people whom he likes."

"Or have eaten," laughed Paul creepily.

"Or eaten," nodded Charles. He looked at them and smiled, then leaned in toward them as if to whisper a secret. "He's never eaten anyone...at least I don't think."

Eevie's smile melted as she turned toward Tommy, his face visibly turning pale.

"What is it?" she asked confused. "Vayne?"

"There's no way Vayne could have tracked us this quickly," said Charles. "This house is protected by very powerful magic."

Then Eevie saw him: the ranger. He was staring directly at the waterfall.

Eevie turned to Charles. "That's Maleficum, the man who tried to kill us!"

"I know Maleficum," said Charles, setting his jaw. "Paul, it looks like we have a surprise visitor—you know what to do."

Paul darted into a darkened hallway, soundlessly disappearing into the shadows.

Standing behind Charles, Eevie and Tommy watched in horror as the ranger spoke a spell, then passed through the waterfall. Moments later, the giant stone wall slid open, and Maleficum limped into Charles's home, an evil grin on his face.

"You have a lot of nerve showing up like this, Maleficum...," Charles's voice was loud and powerful.

"I see you're watching over my two friends," hissed Maleficum, his evil black eyes feeding on their fear.

Charles walked forward, stopping inches from Maleficum's face. Suddenly, Charles threw his arms around his shoulders. "Welcome, my friend," Charles said, embracing him. "It's been too long."

"What?!" Eevie cried out, flabbergasted.

She and Tommy edged backwards. Tommy tripped over Paul, falling heavily to the floor. Paul turned with a look of disgust toward Tommy. "Tsk, tsk. Not such a warrior now," he sneered pretentiously.

Paul turned to Maleficum and smiled. "Welcome back, my dear old friend. We've missed you."

Epilogue

DREW SPILLS THE BEANS

Drew knew it would come to this, and now as he looked out his bedroom window, he could see two police officers walking up his icy sidewalk to his house. Even though he expected the knock, it still jolted his heart as they pounded on the door and shouted, "Police! Open up."

Soon, Drew sat alone in the back of a police cruiser at the Donut Shack. *Deny everything,* he told himself. *You have no idea what happened to Eevie and Tommy, but you'll help however you can.*

Drew shivered. *They could have at least left the heat on for me.* The door to the Donut Shack opened, and only one officer exited—*this can't be good.* Officer Robert opened the back door and leaned his head in.

"Drew, come inside. Mr. Webb, the manager, has something interesting he'd like you to see."

Officer Robert stood behind the car door as Drew climbed out.

"This would be much easier, son," he said, turning to Drew as they walked toward the Donut Shack, "if you would just tell the truth."

Drew's heart sank. He had a sick feeling in his stomach about what was about to go down.

Officer Robert led Drew down a hallway to a door with a small placard that read "Office." The office was tiny, with a small desk, computer, filing cabinet, and bulletin board with various forms and papers. The other officer was leaning over Mr. Webb's desk, watching something intently on his computer.

They looked up as Drew entered the room. Mr. Webb looked like he was extremely uncomfortable. Drew had been a customer at the Donut Shack since he was a young child.

"Hi, Drew," said Mr. Webb, peering over his reading glasses, his bald head shimmering in the florescent overhead light. "The police officers found Eevie and Tommy's bikes behind the dumpster, and we have video surveillance of you with them on the day they disappeared. Drew, please...please tell the officers the truth."

Officer Carl moved Mr. Webb's monitor slightly, allowing Drew to see the black and grainy video of the dining area of the Donut Shack. Drew hung his head low. "It wasn't supposed to happen like this."

"Happen like what?" asked Officer Robert, sternly but kindly.

"Remember when Tommy was attacked a few weeks ago and he escaped through his bedroom window?" Drew said.

The officers nodded. Drew had their rapt attention.

"Well," Drew said, "he recognized the intruder. He said that it was Park Ranger Miller."

"Ranger Miller?" replied Officer Carl. "How did he know Ranger Miller?"

"Why didn't he tell anyone?" asked Officer Robert. "That's a very serious accusation."

"Tommy and Eevie thought that he was behind the mysterious disappearances at Black Hallow Park," Drew said. "Tommy said he threatened them to stay away. They thought if they could sneak into his house...," Drew's voice softened, "...they would get the evidence they needed. The last time I saw them...," his voice cracked, "...they were sneaking into Black Hallow Park."

Drew felt hot tears filling his eyes. "They made me promise I would never tell."

"Drew," said Mr. Webb, gently grabbing his shoulder, "Eevie and Tommy's parents are worried sick about them. They haven't slept for two days."

"I'm so sorry," cried Drew. "That's everything I know."

"Carl," said Officer Robert, addressing his partner, "put in a call to Taylor at dispatch. Tell her to let Drew's parents know that we're taking him to Ranger Miller's station."

******

The trio's shadows clumped together on the ranger's door. The two officers stood side by side in front of Drew. Officer Carl stepped forward and rapped his knuckles sharply on the door. Drew's heart pounded in his chest. He was about to come face to face with the man who had tried to kill Tommy.

"Good evening, officers," said a friendly voice.

"Good evening, Ranger Miller. Do you mind if we ask you a couple questions?" inquired Officer Robert.

"Certainly," he replied while opening the door. "How can I help?"

Drew stared between the two officers, shocked. It was a different park ranger. "Officer Robert," blurted Drew, "that's not the right park ranger."

Drew stepped forward and pointed. "That's him!"

The officers looked up. Just behind Ranger Miller's head hung a picture of another ranger. The ranger turned and looked back at Drew incredulously.

"Son, I'm afraid you've made a mistake. I've been the ranger for nearly six years. That's Ranger Anderson," he said, looking at the picture. "He retired, and I took over as park ranger here at Black Hallow Park. He died last year. He was a good man."

"That's impossible," said Drew, shaking his head in disbelief. "He was here just two days ago. I saw him. I talked to him!"

Ranger Miller looked at the officers, holding his hands open in an *I don't know* gesture. "Son, Ranger Anderson passed away. I spoke at his funeral. He's buried less than a mile from here at Black Hallow Cemetery."

"We're sorry to bother you, sir," said Officer Robert, shaking Ranger Miller's hand.

Robert turned angrily and stared into Drew's eyes. "I'm getting tired of your lies. Carl, if you don't mind, escort Drew to the car. I'm going to call his parents and have them meet us at the station."

"But I am telling the truth!" Drew cried. "He's lying!"

Officer Carl grabbed Drew by the arm. "Come on, kid."

Drew pulled his arm free. The ranger stood in the doorway, a thin smile forming on his lips. "Good luck with him, officers," he laughed, shaking his head.

The ranger narrowed his eyes and crossed his arms. As Officer Carl pulled him away, Drew's jaw dropped open—and his eyes locked on the silver serpent ring glistening on the ranger's finger.

The adventure continues in Book 3

Read a Sneak Peak of the third book of the Quest Chasers series

CHAPTER 1

Tommy's hand shook as he raised it to his head. A hot, viscous liquid oozed between his fingers. *Is it blood?* He struggled to raise up onto his elbows and sit up.

"What happened?" moaned Tommy, shaking his head. His eyes struggled to focus.

"Behold," mocked a crackly voice. "The brave warrior awakes."

"You're okay," said Eevie gently. She placed a reassuring hand on his shoulder. "We're in Mr. Dixon's hideout."

"Am I bleeding?" whispered Tommy.

"No," said Eevie, trying her best not to laugh. "You tried to attack the ranger, and Paul sort of stopped you...with his wooden ladle."

"He smacked me in the head with a spoon?" asked Tommy incredulously. "It felt like a club."

"My mother gave me this spoon," said Paul dramatically, "and you broke it...with your giant forehead." He dipped his broken ladle into a small, bubbling pot of what looked like melted animal fat. He stirred it for a moment, then using the broken ladle, he slathered the sticky goo all over Tommy's face.

"Okay, Paul, that's enough healing salve," said Charles, laughing. "That's enough for his whole body."

Tommy shoved Paul away and slowly got to his feet. "You're telling me that with all of your magical powers you couldn't have just done a spell to fix my head?" exclaimed Tommy angrily.

"Oh sure, mighty warrior," said Paul, jabbing him in the chest with the end of the ladle. "But where's the fun in that?"

"Your spoon's not the only thing that's going to be broken," growled Tommy. "And why is he here?" He jabbed his finger at the ranger. "He tried to kill us."

"Hah," scoffed the ranger, folding his arms across his chest, "humans, always so dramatic."

"Quiet!" hissed Charles, startling both Paul and Tommy.

Charles snapped his fingers and suddenly they were engulfed in darkness. Tommy could hear the old man chanting rhythmically.

A spell, thought Tommy. *Did Vayne find us*? Vayne the evil sorcerer who had been entombed inside a tree under a powerful spell. He'd tricked them into releasing him…and then he'd killed Cassara, the woman that had rescued them and helped them escape, and now, he was close to finding them.

The walls of the cave shimmered, diffused into a silvery mist, and then vanished. They were still there, surrounding them, protecting them, but they were now invisible.

Eevie gasped. The moon cast a white glow across the immense shoulders of the largest man she'd ever seen.

However, when his face turned toward her, she realized she was wrong, he wasn't human.

The creatures face was oval, shaped like a bony egg. A large curtain of flappy flesh hung from its forehead, down to where the bottom of its nose should be. In the center of the fleshy flap, a huge eye moved from side to side.

Ugh, Eevie shuttered. *So creepy!*

Suddenly, a shadow appeared behind the one eyed-creature.

Eevie's eyes met Tommy's. She could tell he was thinking the same thing she was: *What is this thing?* They both knew it was here for one thing, them.

"A soul thief," said the old man's voice inside their heads, reading their thoughts.

A soul thief? Tommy shivered. *I happen to like my soul right where it is.*

The new shadow moved into the moonlight. Tommy sucked air into his lungs. He had never seen such an evil-looking creature.

"It's a death hound," whispered the old man's voice.

Tommy stared at the shadowy creature as it climbed on top of a large outcrop of rock, just beyond the wall of the cave. The beast looked like a heavily muscled, hairless wolf. It turned its head skyward and inhaled deeply, then suddenly it turned its massive head toward Tommy and stared at him—directly at him, with pale-blue eyes.

Does he see me? Tommy's knees buckled. Those eyes—staring directly into his—sent an icy chill down his spine.

A shrill cry shattered the darkness as the death hound began digging at the side of the cave. The soul thief turned his thick, meaty head—his fleshy eye riveted to the spot where the group stood, hidden behind a veil of protective magic.

The creature contorted its face, and then with the slash of his finger, the bottom half of his face ripped open, creating a fleshy mouth. It open and closed, like a fish out of water. The creature moaned as rivulets of mucousy brown saliva oozed from the bloody opening, dripping down his chin and onto his chest.

"*What* is happening?" whispered Eevie, barely able to breathe.

"*He senses your soul,*" whispered an evil voice in her head. It was the ranger, Maleficum! *"It won't be long,"* his voice hissed.

Won't be long for what? thought Eevie.

"*You'll see,*" replied Maleficum's voice. "*You'll see.*"

"Maleficum," whispered Charles sternly, he shook his head. He put a finger to his mouth and motioned everyone over.

"Children, we only have a matter of minutes before they find us. I'm going to try a spell to lead them away."

Charles hurried across the room and grabbed a thin silver box. He placed it on a long, wooden table filled with vials and papers.

Tommy stole a look outside: The soul thief looked like he was about to be sick. He watched as the giant creature swayed from side to side, his muscular arms wrapped across his convulsing belly.

Tommy scrunched up his face. "Uhm…guys, it looks like Goliath is about to—"

Just as everyone turned to look, the soul thief vomited up what looked like black, squiggly gummy worms bathed in gravy.

"—hurl," finished Tommy as he turned away in disgust.

"Oh God," breathed Paul. "We may be too late."

"Where is he going?" asked Tommy, as Paul raced from the room.

"Never mind him," said Charles sharply. "Eevie, come here, quickly child."

Eevie's eyes nearly rolled up in her head when she saw the contents of the silver box.

"What are you going to do with that needle?" gasped Eevie, her voice trembling.

"It's a diamond needle. It will keep your blood pure…, I'll explain later," he added, seeing the confusion in her eyes. "For now," he said, grabbing her left hand, "you will have to trust me."

Eevie nodded. She watched as he separated her ring finger from the other fingers and held it tightly. The tip of her finger swelled red.

"I'm sorry, Eevie, I cannot use magic to numb the pain," Charles said. "Your blood has to be pure and magic-free, or the death hound will smell it."

Eevie nodded and closed her eyes. "Just do it," she whispered.

A sharp, raw, burst of pain raced through her as he pushed the needle deep into her finger to the bone. At any other time, she would scream out in agony, but she bit down hard to avoid a confrontation with the demons. Hot tears streaked down her cheeks.

"I'm sorry, Eevie," Charles whispered. His voice carried with it the weight of a person left with no other option.

He reached into the silver box and removed what looked like a small ball of dough the size of a marble. Eevie watched as he touched the needle to the ball; it immediately became engorged in her blood, turning crimson red.

Charles touched Eevie's finger and whispered, *"Conprimo."* Instantly the wound on Eevie's finger was healed. Surprised, Eevie looked up. "Thank you." Charles simply nodded.

"You okay?" asked Tommy softly, rubbing her shoulder.

"I'm fine," said Eevie, "just...."

Whoosh! Tommy threw his hands over his head and ducked as a beautiful golden bird soared just inches above him, landing gracefully on Charles's outstretched arm.

"Woah, what the…? That's a big bird!" exclaimed Tommy.

No one seemed to notice Tommy's outburst. All eyes were on Charles and the majestic bird, resting on his arm. Its razor-sharp talons were as large as Tommy's hands, encircling completely around Charles's arm. He placed the doughy crimson ball into the palm of his hand, and then held it up to the magnificent bird. "Quickly," Charles whispered, "take this to Devil's Fork."

Without another word, the bird gently secured the ball in its hooked beak and then literally vanished, leaving behind a golden cloud of glittery dust.

Outside the cave, the squiggly, black worms wriggled and twisted against each other until they melted into a slippery, black, gelatinous blob. The soul thief raised a hand and removed his eye from the fleshy flap, hanging from his forehead.

"He just pulled his eye out," Eevie gulped. "What is up with these creatures and their eyes?"

"A small sacrifice," whispered Maleficum. "Don't worry, he'll grow a new one," he smiled evilly, clearly enjoying Eevie's discomfort.

The soul thief's eye rolled from his fingertips to the ground. His chin dropped to his chest, and his head bowed as if in a trance. The black blob oozed across the rock, like molten lava, covering the creature's eye. Moments later, the eye reappeared at the front of the blob, reawakening the soul thief.

From inside the cavern they could hear the whimpering of the death hound as it sat patiently on its haunches, beside its master.

"Here it comes," said Maleficum, his voice eerily calm.

Thank you for reading The Screaming Mummy

Sign up for the latest info on new upcoming books, bonus content, and free giveaways at questchasers.com

We hope you enjoyed reading the second book in the *Quest Chasers* series: *The Screaming Mummy*. If you enjoyed the story, please leave a review on Amazon, Goodreads, or Barnes & Noble. We'd love to hear from you!

Others by Grace and Thomas Lockhaven

If you love Darren Shan's series, then you'll enjoy *The Ghosts of Ian Stanley*. Great for teenagers who enjoy reading paranormal mysteries.

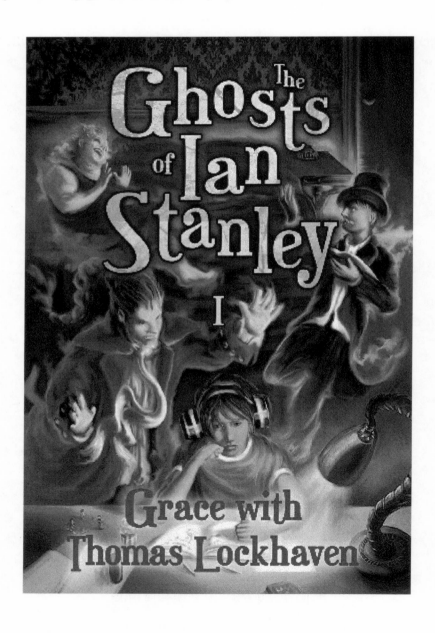

If you love mystery series like Nancy Drew, then you'll enjoy Thomas Lockhaven's *Ava & Carol: Detective Agency* series, perfect for curious-minded 9 to 12-year-old girls.

Book 1: The Mystery of the Pharaoh's Diamonds

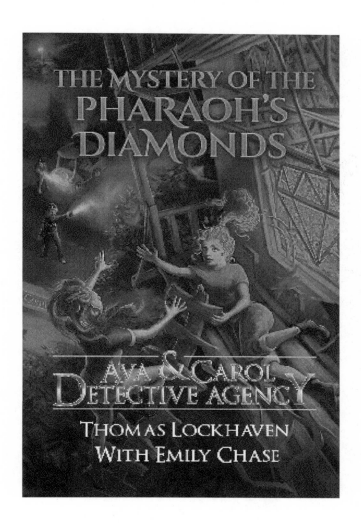

Book 2: The Mystery of Solomon's Ring

Book 3: The Haunted Mansion

Book 4: Dognapped

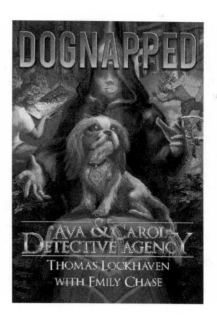

Book 5: The Eye of God

Book 6: The Crown Jewels Mystery

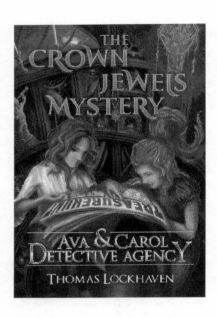

Book 7: The Curse of the Red Devil

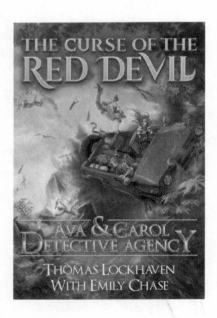

Author T. Lockhaven

Thomas Lockhaven also writes under T. Lockhaven for his adult cozy mystery series. If you love whodunits and amateur sleuths, then you'll enjoy *The Coffee House Sleuths* series.

Book 1: A Garden to Die For

Book 2: A Mummy to Die For

THE COFFEE HOUSE SLEUTHS

T. LOCKHAVEN

2

A MUMMY TO DIE FOR

Book 1: Sleighed (A Christmas Cozy Mystery)

The Coffee House Sleuths

Sleighed

Book 1

T. LOCKHAVEN

Made in the USA
Middletown, DE
26 October 2020